Chapter 1

"Great power brings great responsibility." I read that somewhere years ago. It seems that every so often, somebody remembers something obvious and puts it in print for everyone to ooh and aah over. As for me, I'd known this little fact of life for a particularly long time. I believed it completely. As a result, I often found myself skulking through the darkest, most dangerous parts of the city in the wee hours of the morning, usually in search of a very evil son of a bitch. Granted, that was also my job, but I'd have likely done it anyway.

This time was no different. It had come to my attention that another killer was loose in our city, and it was time for me to do something about it. Oh, I can hear you now, "But there are killings all the time!"

Well, you're right. People die or get killed quite often in Houston. People kill each other for love or money, and I don't lift a finger. Innocents are murdered for their sneakers, and gangbangers kill each other over drugs or turf. People die of neglect, disease, and car wrecks, and though it occasionally pains me to hear of such things, I don't walk the streets at night in an attempt to avert those deaths.

But this particular killer was different. These recent deaths were the work of a single man, one very sick, twisted, and evil individual who brutalized and murdered young women. Now THIS I could do something about, and I would be only too glad to take care of the bastard. Sometimes, humans need a few bad genes removed from the old pool. That's where I come in. My unique talents assist me pretty well in such removals.

Hearing all this, some might ask if I think I'm God. "What right do you have to choose who dies and who lives? What makes you so special?", one might ask. Well, I certainly do not think of myself as God, though I have a lot of his/her power within me. And I actually have far more right to kill than psychos like this one, considering the evil nature of my targets. What goes around comes around. That's a universal law, baby. Most folks would just depend on fate to take care of such karmic debts. Well, just who do you think fate calls on to tend to business? That would be me. I'm a bit special, you could say.

I'm a GrimFaerie.

Although I usually look, walk, talk, and even occasionally think like a man, I am actually far from being human. And don't ever mistake me for one of those cute little winged pixies that flit about and sprinkle shiny dust all over the place. I'm just not that kind of Faerie. And even those are tougher than you think.

No, I'm the kind that had your ancestors bolting their doors and cowering in their homes at night. I'm the kind that caused unwary travelers to disappear in the deepest of our forests without a trace. Seeing me at work is usually enough to send people to years of therapy, and I've heard that their nightmares never go away.

Things have changed quite a bit since I came to be, but some things have always remained

Grim Undertakings

The GrimFaerie Chronicles Book 1

By Whit McClendon

Copyrights

Grim Undertakings
The GrimFaerie Chronicles, Book 1

Copyright © 2019 by Whit McClendon

ISBN-13: 978-1-7326300-4-8
ISBN-10: 1-7326300-4-6

Cover Art by: Wicked Smart Designs
Copyediting by: Michelle McClish
Published by: Rolling Scroll Publishing, Katy, TX
Website: www.jidaan.com

To join my mailing list to be notified when a new novel is published, go to
http://www.whitmcclendon.com/contact

You can also Like my Facebook page!
http://www.facebook.com/whitmcclendonauthor/

Acknowledgements

I'd like to thank all the folks who encouraged me along the way. Writing is a lot of work, but knowing that people out there enjoy my stories makes it much easier. My wife, Christina, has always been super supportive. Thanks to Michelle for her amazing proofing skillz, and Tara for her valuable input as well. And thanks to Brian for almost reading it. Love ya, man.

~Whit McClendon

constant. There has always been evil around. Good and evil, there never is one without the other. Though many might misunderstand me because of my more nasty characteristics and generally bad attitude, I'm actually on the side of Good. When the balance between light and darkness starts to shift in certain ways, the Goddess speaks to me and lets me know when I have a job to do. Like now. I was born as an instrument of higher powers. I just do what my Goddess (your God, or whatever you choose to worship, they're all the same) tells me to do. And I love every minute of it. Especially the bloody stuff.

But I digress. I was following a young woman that was destined to be the killer's next victim. Earlier that day, she had appeared to me in a brief vision, a gift from the Goddess. In that vision, I was made aware of the killer, his past murders, and I got a glimpse of this woman at this place. My mission was clear.

I don't know what she thought she was doing out so late at night. Night is our time, not yours. But then, she was only one of many. More than an hour past midnight, the lights of the many nightclubs on the street called Richmond cast an ever-shifting rainbow of colors on the pools of rainwater in the road. Young humans were everywhere, going from one club to another, most at least mildly inebriated.

Following her had been easy. This woman was a bit taller than most, and a slight shift of my perception showed her to have a bright blue aura, easily distinguishable from the less intense auras of the ordinary humans around her. Their pitiful auras were varied dull shades of reds, yellows, greens, and some blue, but an intense blaze like hers was rare. It marked her as special. Not only did that make my job easier, it also piqued my interest. I wondered what it meant, but then resolved to focus on the job at hand.

Oblivious to the fact she was being tracked, she just walked towards a huge building up ahead. Parking had been horrendous, and she had found a spot for her little vehicle around the corner. I followed her silently, trying to look like just another human out for a night of partying and fun, and I watched her move.

She wore a close-fitting dark blue garment that left her shoulders and midriff bare. A tight skirt of the same color hugged her body and came down to the middle of her thighs. Glints of gold shone around her neck and wrists. As she was on the tall side, I was unsurprised to see flat-heeled shoes on her feet. By human standards, she was probably quite beautiful. The Faerie concept of beauty is somewhat different, but I've lived among humans long enough to gain at least a vague understanding of their varied tastes.

I trailed her at a safe distance, but she never looked back at me. If she had, she would only have seen a medium-sized, dark-haired fellow with green eyes, perfectly ordinary. Just another Saturday night reveler. I grimaced at her lack of awareness. She never once looked to the left or right, only straight ahead, ignoring all others. I pressed on.

Seeing all the humans about made me think that she'd be relatively safe for a while. From what little I knew, the evil one had always abducted his victims, taken them somewhere to do his vile work, and then left the body (or pieces of it) where it could easily be found.   Therefore, nothing truly harmful was likely to happen to her until they reached his killing place, and that was just fine with me. I needed a bit of privacy to do my own work if I wanted to be thorough about it, and I didn't want his screams to draw any attention. His workplace would probably be secluded enough for me. Seeing a GrimFaerie at work would only make any bystanders think that I'm the bad guy, and I didn't want any would-be heroes to try and get in my way.

She continued walking until she reached her destination, a large establishment that went by the name of Avenues. Even from outside, I could hear several different types of music mingling in an awful mess to my Fae ears. It should come as no surprise that human music doesn't thrill me. It's lame. The noise and the energy I felt oozing from the place told me that it was filled to capacity with noisy, drinking, laughing, dancing humans. Not my favorite scene, but you go where the job takes you. Compared to a Faerie Revel, this was a children's party.

The woman walked right up to the beefy doorman and showed him a little card from her purse.   He glanced at it and then smiled appreciatively as he pushed the door open for her. I could see his eyes moving over the lithe muscles of her body as they bunched and moved under her clothing. I stepped forward to follow her, but he quickly barred my way.

"Hey!" The big guy put a massive paw on my chest to keep me still. "I'll need to see...some..." His voice trailed away as I touched his mind. No sparkly dust or fancy words here. Like many of the Faerie, I have the gift of enchantment, the ability to make humans see, think, and feel however I wish them to. I can't force them to actually do anything. That's against the rules. However, I can certainly make a human want something so badly that they'll do anything to get it. I can make suggestions that seem imperative in the moment. And I can make them see what I want them to see. It works wonderfully.

Nothing so complicated was necessary with...Brad. I touched his mind only briefly, leaving a strong impression that he had already seen my little card and that I was to be shown every possible courtesy. It makes it easier for me to work if I don't scare people to death all the time.

"Uh," Brad spoke again, "Sorry 'bout that. Here you go, man!" He pushed open the door and thunderous noise whumped through the open portal, buffeting me. I slipped inside, my eyes instantly adjusting to the semi-darkness. Stairs to my left led up and away to another area, and the more brightly lit piano bar was to my right. The hallway ahead angled away from me, and it was from there that the bulk of the noise was emanating.

The girl was nowhere in sight. I shifted my perception again and watched as the shadowy figures of young men and women suddenly sprang to life in vivid colors. At first, I didn't see her, but I did catch a faint trace of her dazzling blue essence on the air, like the lingering scent of a passing woman's perfume. Those faint traces led me towards the main room, and once there, I found her easily.

She was already in the middle of the throng, her arms held high in the air, her body moving to the pulsing beat of the music. She danced with no one in particular, and as I watched, she turned away several men who made attempts to dance with her. Apparently, she was there for the noise and not the companionship.

Since my vision from the Goddess had not included a view of the killer, all I could do was wait. He would move on her sooner or later, and once I knew who he was and what he looked like, his life was to be measured in minutes. Several of those would be quite agonizing. I smiled at the thought.

I sensed the young, dark-haired human woman long before she actually walked up to me. As soon as she had begun to look at and think about me, I caught the play of energies that wafted from her. I assumed a non-threatening stance of polite aloofness as she walked over. I didn't want to piss her off, but I couldn't afford to waste time with her. Trysts between Faerie and human were rare, but not unheard of. However, Faerie love was a bit intense, and most humans simply could not handle it. In any event, I had no time for that tonight.

"Wanna dance?" She looked up at me and I could see that she wasn't quite as drunk as the others. A pretty little thing...for a human. Keeping my eyes mostly on the dance floor, I touched her mind as I had the doorman's, and gently suggested that her time would be better spent elsewhere. She cocked her head to one side and said, "Sorry, fella, you're not my type," as if I had been the one to ask her instead of vice versa. I nodded at her and she flounced away to put the move on some other unsuspecting guy. As soon as she left, I felt other eyes upon me as a few more women took notice.

As I said, I had no time for this, so I moved away from the bar, watching the woman on the dance floor as I did so. When I felt the gaze of those other women lessen, I flexed my will and became, for lack of a better word, *dim*. Anyone looking at me now would only see a shadow on the wall unless they already knew that I was there. Being Faerie certainly had its advantages.

I watched her dance for the next two hours, keeping my senses open. Nothing happened except that the humans around me got louder and drunker. I was anxious to find the killer, but nothing I could do would hurry him. As long as she was here in the noisy club, I knew that she'd be safe. The club would close eventually, and in that darkest time of the night, I was certain that the killer would take her.

After dancing constantly and never once making eye contact with another soul, she suddenly decided that it was time for her to leave. There was no warning, she simply stopped dancing in the middle of a song and headed for the hallway and the exit beyond. Glad to be on the move again, I undimmed myself and followed her at a safe distance. Even if she did temporarily vanish from my sight, I knew that the traces of her were easy enough to follow.

She slipped through the exit door, and I came soon after. When I emerged, she was already walking away from the club and down the covered sidewalk that fronted the building. I had expected her to retrace her steps from earlier that night, but the rain that pounded into the earth must have dissuaded her. Instead, she stayed under the protection of the overhang and headed towards lights and laughing voices. The dance club was in the farthest end of a strip center, separated from an all-night coffee shop by a handful of businesses long since closed for the day. Several young male humans were laughing and talking as they leaned against the columns outside the coffee shop. She walked towards them, and I saw her aura tighten, a sign that she was on the defensive.

One of the males, the largest, stepped away from his column, calling to her. I could see his teeth from where I was as he grinned stupidly at her, and immediately his friends also stepped forward.

I knew his swagger all too well. There have been men like him from the dawn of time, and they have all been the same. Big, dumb, predatory...and always in need of an audience. This fellow had it all, and it looked like he had decided that my girl was his target for the night.

I stepped into the shadows behind one of the columns and dimmed myself again. I hated guys like this one. I've killed many of them, but only if the occasion truly warranted it, and this was hopefully not one of those occasions. This punk wasn't the killer that I was after, and he might be preventing me from finding the real threat. I just wanted him gone. For now, though, I watched and waited.

The punk stepped smoothly in front of my girl as she tried to pass the coffee shop. She stopped, keeping her eyes forward, and tried to step around him without making eye contact. He moved where she moved, speaking the mindless words that had been spoken countless times before. I did not have time for this.

As much as I would have loved to tear out the stupid human's throat, I knew that it would be the wrong thing to do. The girl must be allowed to go on about her business as planned so that the killer would be able to make his move. When he did that, I would have him. This punk was just an unforeseen obstacle, and I hoped that she could get around him without my help. I'm not subtle when I get serious, and what I had in mind for Mr. Big Smileypunk would most likely frighten her badly. I remained dim as I started to move closer to them, working my way from column to column, trying to find a way to get her past them without showing myself.

They started to close in on her, encircling her. She still refused to look into Smileypunk's eyes, instead choosing to look straight ahead, imperious, as if her gaze was too important to waste on him. He did not like that.

One big hand reached out to grab her chin, forcing her face towards his. I could not see her face from where I was, but was surprised to see the smile on the punk's face disappear as his buddies burst into laughter. She'd insulted him. Good for her.

I heard him call her a 'bitch', a word I recognized as a bad one, and watched his face quickly flare an ugly red as he raised his right hand to strike her. It looked like I was going to have to step in after all. Good. I hadn't killed anyone in a while, and though I'd prefer to wait for the murderer, this one would do just fine.

It was not to be, though. As the punk whipped his open hand at her, intending to deliver a humiliating slap, she stepped into the blow, blocking his arm with the sharp ridge of her upraised forearm and simultaneously punching him in the throat with her other hand. Before he could even register the pain, she had grabbed him by the arm and shoulder and then slammed a vicious knee into his groin. He buckled, as all human males do when struck there, and his eyes grew wide. Moving smoothly and with far more strength than I thought she had, she yanked him off balance, whirled, then hit him with a judo throw before he had time to recover. He went down hard, bouncing his thick skull on the pavement.

Shocked, the guy's buddies were silent and wide-eyed as they watched this girl climb onto their leader's chest, pin his arms with her knees, and start buffeting his face with powerful palm strikes. His legs stopped kicking on the second shot, but she kept hitting him. It had been many years since I'd seen that kind of ferocity from a human female. I smiled.

One of the remaining males made the mistake of grabbing her hair. She was up in an instant and struck him a blow in the gut that made him go pale and release his grip. She punched him in the throat and kicked out at another man's knee, bringing them both down at once. The whole thing took only a handful of frantic seconds. Her viciousness apparently had startled the other two thugs enough that they were having trouble deciding what to do.

In that moment, she burst into motion, sprinting down the walkway and leaving three injured men behind her. A big grin slid across my face as I watched her go. I love it when the bad guys get theirs.

"Get her!" one man croaked even as he clutched his injured knee. He'd not be running anytime soon, but the two idiots who were left uninjured took off after the fleeing woman. Whatever they planned on doing to her when they caught her would definitely not be good. It was time for me to act.

Still dim, I stepped out into the parking lot so I would have room to move. The rain would not bother me, and in fact I welcomed it. We Faerie are not worried about a little water, and it would hide me from their feeble human eyes until I wished otherwise.

I could see that the woman was just reaching the end of the covered walkway and was about to sprint across the parking lot towards the street beyond. The punks were gaining on her, but I was not worried. I had plenty of time to reach them.

In addition to being stronger, smarter, and possessed of many interesting abilities, the Faerie are also blessed with great speed. It came in handy quite often. I used mine and the world became a blur around me. A heartbeat later I was standing in the shadows behind the last column along the walkway, listening to the two thugs' shoes loudly slapping the pavement as they approached. They had no idea just how close they were to death.

But then, I really was not there to kill those men. Although they were definitely in need of a good thrashing, killing them would bring the police, who would only complicate things. I didn't need that, so I decided to let them live.

I stepped out in front of them, mere yards away, and undimmed myself. They were startled to see a man appear as if by magick, but they could not stop so suddenly. I knew that. I crouched a bit and revealed my true self to them. Their faces went white as they frantically started to backpedal, desperate to escape me. They need not have worried that much. At least, not this time.

I lashed out and struck each one in the head, enjoying the feel of it, but keeping my claws to myself. Both men lost consciousness immediately and their bodies pitched past me like rag dolls as their momentum carried them towards the unyielding asphalt. I dimmed myself again and turned to see my girl racing across the street, disappearing between two parked vehicles. Her aura was still easily visible to me. Rain doesn't affect such things.

I turned the unconscious thugs face-up and knelt between them so I could see their faces. With the briefest of touches, I entered their minds and impressed upon them that it would be unwise for them to continue to antagonize others. If they did it again, I would know of it. I would come for them in the night, and my wrath would be far worse this time. I left the faintest hint in their minds of the possible consequences, and their sleeping faces twitched as the nightmares began.

I reached out with one hand and traced my claws across the face of each man, just hard enough to draw blood. The scars would be fade in time, but the memories would last forever. They would avoid this part of town like the plague.

I had indulged myself long enough, so I looked out towards the street, searching for the trail of my girl. It was there, fading now, but still easily visible to my Faerie sight. I caught sight of the tail end of it, a wispy mist that dissipated even as I watched. It wound between a pair of silent vehicles and into a parking lot on the far side of the street. The rain did not affect it at all, but as auras don't stick around forever, I sprinted after it, and the girl that left it.

Before I could lay eyes on her again, I heard her scream. It was a short, startled yelp, followed by the sound of flesh striking flesh. From her, I heard nothing more. Then I heard the door of a van slam shut, and I knew I was too late. While I had been fooling around with the locals, he had made his move. Dammit.

Just as I spotted the plain black van, its motor growled to life. It burst into motion, quickly, but not recklessly enough to draw much attention, especially at such a late hour. It moved down the street away from me, its crimson taillights glaring like a demon's eyes, rapidly leaving me behind.

That pissed me off.

Glancing quickly around, I was pleased to see that the street was mostly deserted, so what I was about to do probably wouldn't end up on YouTube. I burst into a run, dimming myself as I did so. I'm capable of incredibly high speed, but I can't maintain it for too long. Even I get tired. The van turned right at a corner up ahead and I was relieved to see that the building on that block was only one story. I angled my pursuit so that I approached the structure at the nearest corner and leaped high into the air to land on its roof. Dodging the blocky air conditioning units, I sped across the top of the building and skidded to a stop at the far side. The van had turned its lights off as soon as it had exited the street, and now tooled along the service drive behind a row of deserted shopping centers. I paralleled its course by following along the rooftops of the adjacent buildings, keeping an eye on the van as I went. Occasionally, I had to leap up another story or two to reach the next roof, but now that the van had slowed, that was easy. I kept the prowling vehicle in sight.

I had a suspicion where the van was headed, and I turned out to be correct. All of my night skulking had left me with a pretty thorough layout of

Houston in my head, and I knew there was a huge, empty lot nearby that was bordered on all sides by trees and unkempt bushes. The store that had once been there had burned to the ground years ago, and after being demolished to its naked slab, had never been rebuilt or repurposed. There was ample cover there this time of night. That would be the kill site.

At least this time, the victim would be the killer rather than the girl. I smiled at the thought. I love my work.

Sure enough, the van entered the lot and hugged the side of the building, shielded from even the wan glow of the nearest streetlights. Fortunately, I could see even in the darkness of the moonless night; it was plain as day to my eyes. The van stopped and the engine quieted. The van shuddered slightly from movement inside, but no noise came from within, and it quickly stilled once more.

I placed one hand on the rim of the building's roof and lightly vaulted over the edge. Rain still came down in a steady drizzle that would have masked any sounds I made as I landed in a crouch on the concrete below, just a few yards from the van. I watched and waited, but nothing moved. Then, as I stood up and began to close the distance to the van, I heard a scream, though it was quickly muffled. The van began to show signs of a struggle, rocking jerkily on its shocks as conflict erupted inside. Without hesitation, I punched my fingers into the seam of the van's side door and, with one ferocious yank, wrenched the door from its hinges and flung it away.

There, revealed in the dim glow of the van's interior lamp, a large man in dark sweats was kneeling over the woman I had followed. She was bound at wrists and ankles, but that had not stopped her from lashing out violently and constantly at her assailant as he tried to restrain her. The man had light hair and was bulkier than the young toughs in the parking lot, but that didn't concern me. Maybe it should have. In the next heartbeat, he whipped his head towards me, assessed the threat, and then backhanded me across the face with enough force that it would have killed me, had I been human. As it was, it flung me several feet away to fall flat on my back on the rain-pelted concrete, momentarily stunned. Without a backward glance, he returned his attention to the struggling girl on the floor of the van.

Friends, I have walked this earth a long time. I've fought with creatures living, dead, and somewhere in between, the likes of which would kick the crap out of crowds of ordinary humans, and chuckle all the while. I've killed things that would give lions and tigers and bears good reason to run and hide. The guy in the van was human, I was certain. But his power was far beyond anything that mortal man should have been able to achieve. My jaw even ached a little.

This was getting good.

I got to my feet and launched myself at the man, unleashing more of my Faerie strength than I had in a long while, slamming him into the opposite side of the van and leaving a large impression of his face in the sheet metal. Before he could recover, I yanked him off of the girl and out of the van. The impact had stunned him, but he regained his composure with surprising speed. Before I could reset, he managed to get one of his huge mitts up to my chin and he pushed, much harder than I expected. He drove my head up and back for just an instant, and that was long enough for him to break free of my grip. I'm fast, like crazy fast. It's just how I'm made. He shouldn't have been able to get through my guard like that, but the next thing I felt was a Herculean blow to my midsection. Having felt a punch from the actual Big-H himself, I had a basis for comparison, and this guy was close. The force of the blow drove me back a couple of steps as I caught my balance. He swung again, but I had his measure now, and I slipped it easily, as well as the nasty uppercut that followed it. Taking advantage of the opportunity, I lunged forward and slammed my forehead straight into his face. I felt the bones crunch under the impact, and I smiled at the sensation. It was nice.

He staggered back, his hands clutching his ruined face, but I could see that he was already recovering. I shook my head in appreciation. Whatever this guy was on was incredibly potent. He might not even be feeling pain. I had to do something to shut him down. I decided to use the biggest weapon I could think of: Mother Earth.

I stepped forward, gripped his thick sweatshirt in both hands and twisted sharply, bringing him over my shoulder and then slamming him down face first into the concrete at my feet. The impact was tremendous, and cracks spread out like the spokes of a spiderweb beneath his limp body. Whatever fight had been in him before had instantly dissipated when he lost consciousness.

I reached for his throat with my clawed fingers, but then stopped short of ripping him open. I had questions. He couldn't answer them if he was dead. I looked in the van and spied a bag of thick zip ties next to the still-struggling girl. I snatched it up and proceeded to bind his wrists and ankles in as awkward a position as I could manage. I made his bonds unreasonably tight, and smiled while I did it. Didn't want him breaking loose. I left him there, face down and bleeding in the rain.

The girl in the van had managed to sit up, and her eyes were wide with both fear and anger. I could sense her defiance. It wafted from her, a scent as easily discernable to a Faerie like me as freshly baked bread. She was no easy mark, this one. Her eyes were on me and I could see puzzlement. Then I realized that I had yet to undim myself, so I likely appeared as a man-sized shadow in the rain. I let that part of my glamour fall away as I slowly approached the van.

"Who are you? Who was that bastard?" Her lips were clamped into a tight line of anger. I raised my hands to show that I was unarmed and that I meant no harm. I allowed my voice to be as calming as possible, a gentle but effective magick.

"No idea. I just saw the van acting weird so I checked it out. Glad I could help. You OK?" She visibly relaxed at the sound of my voice. Score another one for the Faerie.

"Give me a second and I will be." She wiggled to a better seated position, raised her bound hands over her head and then brought them down sharply towards her lap, spreading her elbows apart as she did so. The zip ties popped apart, and she was free. Just like that. She rubbed her wrists for a few seconds and then started working at the ties on her ankles with her fingers. She looked around the floor of the van for a few seconds, picked up a wicked looking dagger, and efficiently slashed through the plastic. "Oh, yeah, that's better."

She was still afraid, deeply so. I could feel her fear. But her determination was far stronger than her fear. That was unusual for a human. Very unusual. I started to like her then. She tossed the knife back into the van, but I caught a better look at it as it left her fingers, and something about it struck me as familiar. And dangerous. I slowly stepped closer and offered her my hand.

"Here, let me help you out of there. We've got to get the cops to come get this guy." Of course, I could care less about the police, but it seemed the thing to say. She accepted my hand and stepped out of the van. Her eyes widened as she got a better look at me, but she said nothing more. She winced as she moved around, but she had no major injuries that I could sense. She was going to be black and blue in the morning, but for now, she seemed all right. I leaned in and snagged the knife from the floor of the van, holding it away from her so she wouldn't think I was going to use it on her. People get a bit paranoid after being kidnapped and assaulted, and I wanted her to feel safe with me.

"That knife looks weird. Old." Her voice shook slightly as the rain's chill began to seep into her. She was right, though. The knife was ancient, a thousand years or more. Its blade was razor sharp and nearly a foot long. Wicked looking runes were inscribed along the blade and on the crossguard. The handle looked to be gold wrapped in leather, and a single ruby was embedded in the end of the pommel. I'd seen thousands of knives, but this one was special. Almost unique. It was one of a set of 6. I had thought that I'd gotten them all over the centuries, but apparently, this one had been stolen from its keepers somehow. That was extremely bad, as this was a knife used specifically to summon things. Bad things. It had taken thousands of lives, all of them in terror and agony. The handle had an oily feel to it, and it made my hand ache as I held it. Not good.

"It is. Old and dangerous. I'll save it for the cops." I quickly searched the van and found a newly made scabbard for the dagger. I sheathed it and tucked it behind my belt. I had no intention of turning it over the cops, of course. No, I planned to take care of that blade personally.

As I stepped out of the van, we both heard the distinctive popping sounds of zip ties being broken. Apparently, the bad guy knew that trick too. I turned my head in his direction only to see him cutting though the ties on his ankles with a pocketknife. In jerky, unsteady movements, the guy got to his feet, swaying as he struggled to stay upright. He was standing all wrong, his head lolling sideways on a neck that was obviously broken. Blood dripped from the corner of his mouth, and I could see that his eyes were not tracking quite right. I guess I slammed him a little too hard. Whoops.

Suddenly, the atmosphere around us thickened. The hairs rose up on our arms and a feeling of dread settled on us both. The raindrops suddenly just stopped, frozen in the air as time ceased to flow. Where there had not been one before, a Presence had arrived, and it was powerful. The girl instinctively stood closer to me, though I could tell that she was ready to flee or fight, depending on what needed doing.

"You won this round, Faerie," his voice was raspy and deep. And he knew what I was. Shit. "But you won't be so lucky next time. Your kind will bow before me. The prophecy will be fulfilled, you will drown in rivers of blood, and this world will be mine. MINE." Without further ado, he drew the pocketknife across his neck, spraying blood in a fountain down his chest. The girl beside me grabbed my arm in shock, but otherwise didn't make a sound. The dead man stood there for a moment, his lifeblood burbling through the slash at his throat. Then he fell to his knees and pitched face down on the concrete. Suddenly, the pressure in the air was gone, and the rain pattered on the ground just as it always had, as it was meant to.

We were silent for a few moments there, together in the rain. Although I was used to such otherworldly things, she was not. And truth be told, this felt a bit bigger than my usual pay grade. I was going to have to dig into this, like right now. I could feel the dagger safely stowed at my back. That was the place to start. That's when she spoke again.

"You're of the Faerie? The dream said you would be. Wow, that's awesome! Wanna go to my place so we can talk?"

It took a moment for me to realize what she had said.

Something was out there stirring up the dark powers. Something big. The night had suddenly become far more dangerous than I had expected, and more interesting. Definitely more interesting.

Chapter 2

In the cold and dark, the thing moved, coiling around itself as best it could. There was no light here, no warmth, but over the millennia, the thing had not only become accustomed to the darkness and cold, but had come to relish it. Where once it had been of the Light, it was now Darkness personified, nothing but a swirling cloud of evil held together by an intense will and focus that had long since passed into madness. Completely insane, yet ferociously intelligent, the being plotted and planned, as it had for centuries upon centuries. Events had finally come to a convergence, and at last the great game would be won. Freedom was close, tantalizingly close. For one who had waited for so long, another few days were as nothing.

Through one of the tiny conduits it had created into the material world, it felt the shock and pain as one of its avatars was broken upon a hard surface. Its pitiful neck had been snapped. The darkness writhed in anger as it sensed one of the Faerie involved. *One of the Grims,* it muttered to itself in a language lost to all but an immortal few. *No matter, I have more creatures, more pieces to move in this game.* It made its puppet dance, spoke through it with the intent of unnerving the Faerie. Through vast distance in both time and space, the thing sensed the Faerie's dismay, its sudden apprehension.

The darkness laughed.

Chapter 3

I followed the girl back to her little car, one I recognized as a Mini Cooper, and watched as she unlocked it with a tiny device. The car chirped in welcome and she quickly got inside. The door on my side popped open and I could see her leaning over towards me, beckoning.

"Come on, get in!" she called. "If there's another guy like that out here, I don't want to meet him!"

I glanced around, but saw and sensed nothing. The rain continued to fall, dampening my ability to hear and see as far as I ordinarily might, and I had to agree; retreating was a great idea. Without a word, I slid into the passenger seat and shut the door. Although I knew that I would survive anything short of a massive explosion (and even that would be hard-pressed to kill me completely), I reflexively clicked the seatbelt into place. No sense in being reckless. "Where are we going?"

She cranked up the engine and put the car in gear. Flashing a grin, she replied, "I told you before, I'm taking you to my place. It's a little ways from here, but I think you'll like it. So you're of the Faerie?"

Wow, she didn't beat around the bush, this human. Good. From what I could tell, this was going to be a fast and crazy ride, and I might not have time to hold her hand and gently introduce her to what I am. The Goddess had sent me to find this girl, and she wouldn't have done that without good reason. The fact that she seemed to be more than she appeared at first glance had to mean something. "Yes, I am. I'm a Grim. We are...keepers of the balance."

"You're an assassin." It was a statement, not a question, and I turned an appraising glance towards her. Her expression was one of both determination and eagerness. The attempted kidnapping and possible murder hadn't fazed her one bit. This one knew more than most, maybe more than she should have. From what I had already seen, it looked like she could handle herself better than most humans, so I decided to be honest with her. To a point. Most of my work was on a definite need-to-know basis, and although she seemed good for it, I'd only just met her.

I turned my gaze back to the windshield and watched the road ahead. After some efficient driving on her part, we ended up on I-10 headed west, away from the city.

"In a manner of speaking, yes. I think of myself more as a trouble-shooter for the Goddess. I go where she tells me, and I do what needs doing. Often, it gets messy, but that's the way of things. And I'm good at it."

She chuckled. "Ha! I'll bet you are!" Her smile was bright under the passing streetlights. "You tossed that guy around like he was nothing, and he was a moose."

I said nothing at that. He was nothing at all like a moose, though he was, indeed, bigger than most humans. But then, I'd long since learned that humans have odd manners of speech. The silence stretched for a few minutes as I contemplated what to say and do next. Fortunately, the girl seemed content with my reticence for the time being, so I just kept my eyes on the road, not really seeing any of it as I contemplated my options.

We drove in silence for a while. She occasionally made comments to herself as she navigated, but that didn't bother me. She finally took an exit just past Katy, then turned on a road going north. She turned a few more times, and each time, the road she chose was narrower and in worse condition than the last. We were leaving the city lights behind, heading towards an area that had yet to be taken over by the constantly growing sprawl of suburbia.

Out here, the stars were still bright and the night was silent. Gone was the oppressive sense of claustrophobia that accompanied so many people living so close together. I had long since learned to shut it off, living as I had in the middle of town, but it was a relief to be among the trees and have empty sky above me for a change. I relaxed slightly as she turned onto a gravel road that led off into a thickly wooded area farther north. I felt a sharp pang of longing for the immense forests I had roamed in my youth, centuries ago. The trees here were tall and beautiful, but nothing like the titanic boles I had known back in the day. Those forests were dark and dangerous, so very alive with life and magick. The unwary could be swallowed up in heartbeats by creatures both magickal and mundane. Most of the forests here were window gardens by comparison.

"Where are we?" I finally spoke. I'm sure my voice was sterner than she had expected, and I felt her tense beside me.

"I'm taking you to my house. Well, it was my mother's before, but it's mine now. I'm all that's left of the Family." Something in her tone interested me. She wasn't referring to her family the same way as I had often heard other humans do. There was an emphasis on 'family' that I found intriguing. I had a feeling that all would be made clear in time, so I said nothing more.

The road had become little more than a one-lane gravel path, and the trees on either side obstructed my view of the sky. Something itched on the edge of my perception, and I suddenly came to full alert. Whatever it was, it wasn't good. "We need to hurry. I think something approaches."

"Almost there, just hold your horses." True to her word, she guided the car out of the trees and into a clearing that covered a square acre or so. A huge wooden house dominated the center of the plot, with a barn and a couple of other small buildings standing silently nearby. It was an old farmhouse, by the look of it, two stories with a wrap-around porch. Lights burned merrily in a few of the windows.

And as we approached the barn, I felt the faint hum of magick in the air. Not from whatever was approaching, but from the house itself.

This night just kept getting more and more interesting.

She pulled the little car into the open door of the barn, and I noted that there was a larger vehicle covered with a tarp inside, as well as a motorcycle in a stall that had once housed a horse at some point. Other stalls had been neatly boarded up, creating individual rooms with closed doors, obviously far removed from any real farming.

The girl parked the Cooper and we both got out. I inhaled the familiar country smells of earth, sky, and flower, mingled with old wood and the scent of animals long gone. It was good to get out of the city stink after being there for so long. I wasn't made to live like that, and I let the sensations wash over me for a moment, refreshing me.

That's when I heard the screeching.

"Shit! Come on!" She grabbed my hand and pulled me towards the house, obviously not knowing that I was far faster than she could ever be. I let her pull me out of the barn and then slipped out of her grasp so that I could turn and see what was coming. In my heart, I already knew. A screech pierced the night, followed by another a little ways off. There were two of them.

"What are you doing? Come on, I said! You don't understand!" She grabbed me by the shoulder and tried to pull me towards the house, but I could not be budged. My eyes were on the threat above. A low growl escaped me and I flexed my knees into a crouch, planning the best way to attack when they got close enough.

High above us, they appeared as darker shadows against the night sky, their quick and agile forms blotting out the stars as they passed. Two pairs of glowing red eyes betrayed their presence, though I could see far more of them with my Faerie sight. I named the threat at last.

"Gargoyles. Dammit." Their hides consisted of hard stone, making my job much, much harder than it might have been. My claws were nothing compared to theirs, huge as they were and sprouting from both their massive hands and prehensile feet. Oh, did I mention their fangs? Jaws strong enough to bite off a man's head in one chomp. I could hear their wings flapping up there as they circled us. The attack would be swift, and they'd both attack at once.

Suddenly, I felt a hard slap against the side of my face. Then another. I raised an eyebrow and turned towards the distraction only to find the girl winging another slap my way. I caught it and held her arm there. "WHAT?"

"You can't fight them, I know that! Get to the porch, right now, you asshole!" Without another word, she turned and sprinted for the house. I blinked at her for a moment, then decided that it was possible, just possible, that she knew something that I did not. The sound of wings above me, followed by a throaty bellow that I recognized as a war cry, finally helped me make my decision.

I, too, sprinted for the house, ending up on the porch before she had taken five running steps. Apparently, that pissed off the gargoyles. They had wanted to enjoy messing with me a bit before killing me. I know their type. Hell, I *am* their type.

They dove hard and fast at the girl instead. I could see their wide open mouths, anticipating a fresh bloody meal. As she stepped on the porch, she reached out and slapped a palm-sized square of what looked like granite, embedded in one of the wooden columns that supported the roof. Instantly, I felt a powerful surge of magick, and the gargoyles slammed into an unseen barrier that flashed blue as they hit it. I'm pretty sure that one of them broke a tooth. They slid into a heap on the ground as if they had fetched up against a transparent, yet unbreakable, wall. They were only stunned for a moment, tough bastards that they were. They shook off the blows and got to their feet, glaring at us as we stared back at them. Only a few feet separated us, but we seemed to be safe behind the mystical barrier.

"Yeah, up yours, Stoneface! Can't get me here, this land is MINE!" she vigorously extended both middle fingers at the pair, who continued to glare at us as she hurled some rather colorful insults their way. If the girl's defiance bothered them at all, they made no sign of it. The two creatures spoke to each other in their own deep, rumbling language, as if deciding what to do. Moments later, they turned and took to the sky again, their huge, bat-like wings flapping loudly in the night air. In moments we were alone, and the only sounds were those of the wind in the trees and the faint singing of the night birds. "Yeah, that's right, you'd better run," she said over her shoulder as she turned, unlocked the front door, and walked inside.

Against my better judgement, I was really getting to like this girl.

Chapter 4

"What do you mean, 'she escaped?'"

On the highest floor of the Bress Tower downtown, Elias Bress fought to control the anger in his voice. He sat behind a massive mahogany desk. His hands were clasped as if in prayer before his face as he strove to remain calm. Bottle-green eyes glared over his entwined fingers at the looming creatures before him. They narrowed, revealing his frustration. The two gargoyles stood silently, their stony skin giving off a musty smell in the usually lemony-pine scented suite. Their faces betrayed no fear, though their clawed hands clenched and unclenched in agitation and they lowered their gaze as their master spoke. Their service to him was not voluntary, and his chastisement was reluctantly tolerated only by necessity.

"She's just a girl! She's nothing! First, she escapes my best man, Luther, and then she gets away from you two as well?" Leaning slightly forward in his frustration, Elias Bress pressed the heels of his strong hands against the ache that had begun at his greying temples. Otherwise jet-black hair, cut stylishly short at the most expensive barber Elias could find, framed a face that might have been handsome if not for the cold anger that shone out from it. He was clean-shaven, with a dimple in his square chin that made some think he looked like an old-school superhero. Or a villain. "Great gods below, this is not the time for such nonsense. I've managed to make this look like the work of a crazed serial killer up to now, but it looks like I'll have to resort to more brutish methods." Taking a deep breath, he leaned back in his chair and regarded the silent creatures once more. They stood impassively waiting for new orders. Elias sighed. This unfortunate course of events had not been foreseen, not at all. And that bothered him immensely.

"Never mind, never mind. I'll deal with it. All right, then. You," he pointed to one of the gargoyles, "you go and clean up Luther's mess. Bring his body to me, and don't forget the dagger. I should never have trusted him with it anyway." He looked at the other stone being. "And you...you go and keep a watch on her house. If she leaves alone, then just snatch her up and bring her to me. Otherwise, report her movements. Now, go." With a shooing motion, he dismissed them and watched them walk out of the sliding glass doors to the wide patio outside and into the gentle drizzle that still fell out of the darkened sky. They spread their wings gracefully for such bulky and strong creatures, then they caught the wind and flew silently into the night. Elias stood up and walked outside after them, ignoring the light rain that slowly dampened the shoulders of his expensive suit jacket. He placed his hands firmly on the wet railing and looked out over the benighted city. At this height, he could see for miles in all directions. He often walked out on the balcony at night, letting the distant city sounds and the soft lights of downtown soothe him as he contemplated some thorny problem or other.

Tonight, though, there was no comfort to be found in the cool air. The alignment was rapidly approaching, and his chance, his one chance, would be lost forever unless he had the girl. She was the key to it all. Unlimited wealth. Power. Everything he could ever desire would be his, but the girl had to die, and soon, or else the opportunity would be lost. Elias looked up into the rumbling clouds, lit from within by flashes of grey lightning. The approaching cloud cover obscured the stars, but he knew their configuration by heart. The stars and planets would not be aligned like this for another five thousand years, and he knew that time was running out. It was to be either her soul...or his.

Chapter 5

"You're a witch?"

She came out of the kitchen with two bottles of beer in one hand and a metal bottle opener in the other. She set one bottle down on a low coffee table, opened hers with one deft movement, and tossed the cap on the table before flopping into an old but comfortable-looking chair. It had taken her only a few minutes to slip out of her tight little clubbing dress and into a mismatched set of baggy sweats. She put one foot up on the table and crossed the other on top of it as she brought the bottle to her lips and drank thirstily from it. She stifled a burp, and nodded. "Yeah, you could say that. I mean, we're not the granola-crunching, cloak-wearing, glitter-farting bunch you see at the ren faires. We do real magick." A dark look crossed her face then and she paused before continuing. "I mean I...I do real magick. It's just me, now."

I looked around the room, allowing her to deal with her momentary pain. I figured I'd hear the story when she was ready to tell it. The home was cozy and warm, its floor covered with thick rugs over wood planking. The furnishings were country and comfortable, with soft couches and chairs, old cherrywood furniture, and pictures on the walls. I walked closer to one of them and found my gaze drawn to the two figures behind the glass. Wearing tiny denim shorts and a flowery shirt, a child-sized version of the girl across from me was standing next to a woman who shared almost the same face, though it had a certain slyness to it that I found instantly appealing. Her hair was darker than the girl's, and longer, and she was far curvier than the woman her daughter would grow up to be. I found myself wondering what kind of woman she had been to have raised the tough, capable girl who now sat with one leg draped over her chair across from me, drinking a beer. I might have liked her.

"Interesting," I broke the silence. I had come across many who used the title of 'witch,' most of whom had no idea what being a true witch was about. True witches were tough in ways that the dabblers couldn't even begin to understand. Magick took a ton of discipline. The world of Faerie, the ways of magick, none of it had a damn thing to do with that Walt Disney guy. He didn't know what the hell he was talking about. Snow White was bullshit. The evil Queen, though...she had been real. And far more beautiful and terrifying than any cartoon could begin to portray. It had been fun to rip her heart out, but then, she had deserved it. "Your family followed the Path?"

"Yeah, we did." Her voice had steadied. "And I still do. My mom raised me in it, taught me everything I know. Like how to raise a shield around the house to keep the uglies out. Nothing that's not human can get in here."

"But I'm in," I countered. "I'm not human."

"You were already in when I cast the thing," she explained. "And you had my permission. Intent is everything, you know. Now then," she focused a rather direct stare at me. "What exactly is a Grim? I know a little, but it's been a long time since Mom told me about your kind."

I answered her question with one of my own. "What's your name?"

"Ha!" She barked a laugh. "I may not know everything, but I know damned good and well that I'm not telling you my true name!"

I smiled. There's power in a name, quite a lot of it. Think about every time you hear your name. It sends a thrill through you, doesn't it? And there's a certain way that you, and only you, say your name when asked. See, there's far more power in that sequence of syllables than you'll ever know. You can be enslaved by the right spell used in conjunction with the perfect and proper pronunciation of your name. If folks knew the things I could do with that kind of information, with the sound of their true name spoken just so, they'd shit their pants. At least, they would if I ordered them to. The fact that she knew it was a good thing, especially if we were going to be dealing with creatures from the magickal realm.

She leaned back in her chair with a grin and continued. "It's OK, Mom gave me enough names that no one will ever get them all right. The short version is Ariana Rhodes; you can call me Ariana. Now what about you, handsome? What do I call you?"

I've been called by many names over the centuries. Many of them, not so nice. Several of them were nearly unpronounceable. Obviously, I wasn't going to give her anything resembling my own, true name.

"You can call me Kane."

"Kane," she said, and I could see her turning the name over in her mind. "Doesn't that mean pretty in Welsh or something like that?"

One corner of my mouth turned up in a half-smile. "In that language, it actually means beautiful, but in old Celtic, it means warrior. It's not my true name, but it'll do." Beneath my glamour, I knew that she would find me anything but beautiful. I could make her want me anyway, most certainly, but although I influence humans all the time, it would feel impolite in this case. I was supposed to save her, not bang her.

"All right, Kane," she said, testing out the name. "Why are these things suddenly after me? First that big ape outside the club, and then those two rockheads...I haven't been causing any trouble lately." She cocked her head to the side as she considered. "Well, hardly any. And certainly not enough to warrant that kind of attention." She took another swallow of beer and eyed me steadily. "What's the deal, *Kane*?" She emphasized my name slightly, enjoying poking fun at me.

I thought for a moment, wondering for myself what the deal might be. The vision from the Goddess had not been complete, but then it never was. I was only given enough information to do the job at hand, and in this case, the job had expanded far beyond my usual scope. I just didn't have any real answers for her. Yet. Like she said, I'm an assassin, and a damned good one, I might add. There's an element of detective work in such an occupation, and I had an awful lot of experience. Given enough time, I could run this down. And from what I'd seen so far, she might just be able to help me along the way and survive the process.

Along with that thought came a flash vision, so powerful that it froze me in place. I saw Ariana in my mind's eye, not as she was now, relaxed and draped over a chair, but bloodied and battered. She stood back to back with a taller, shadowy figure, and both were crouched, ready for combat. She had a wicked looking short sword in one hand and the other she held high overhead. In that hand, she clutched something that glowed white-hot, so bright that I couldn't see what it was. Outside the circle of light she cast, I could see hundreds of roiling inhuman shapes, creatures of the deeper darkness. There were glints of fang and claw, and I could hear their hungry growls. Ariana's face was a crimson mask of determination, and I heard her bellow a wordless war cry, egging on whatever stood outside the circle of her light. Just then, the taller figure looked over its shoulder and her light caught its bloodied face so that I could see it. It was mine. My true face.

"Hey...hey, you all right?" Her voice snapped me out of the vision. The Goddess hadn't been very forthcoming, but I knew a freaking sign when I saw one. Whatever this mess was, Ariana was deeply involved in it, and not just a random victim as I had thought at first. She was going to have to come with me and fight this thing, and it was going to get messy.

"Yes," I croaked. "Yes, I'm fine. Have you got anything to eat? We've got a lot to talk about, and I'm hungry."

"I thought the Faerie couldn't eat our food?" she asked as she stood up out of her chair and wandered towards the kitchen.

"No, that's backwards. You can't eat *our* food. We can eat yours all we want." And I was going to need a lot of fuel for whatever lay ahead.

*   *   *   *   *   *

The visions only gave me a limited amount of information. No matter how powerful and arresting they were, I could only learn so much. I had to figure out where these attacks were coming from. "Hey, is that shield still up around the house? I need to check on something."

She wiped her mouth with a paper towel, removing the dab of mustard that had somehow escaped while she was eating her sandwich. "Hell yeah, it is. It's going to be up all the time until this mess is over with. What do you want to check on?"

"Here, follow me." I made my way back through to the front of the house, out the front door, and onto the porch. I could feel the tingle of magick much stronger so close to the spell that kept the house safe. She came up behind me as I scanned the ground in front of the porch, and I pointed at a tiny object that lay just beyond the shield boundary.

"There. I need that." I turned to look at her and she stared back at me with a worried look.

"Um...OK, but hurry up and get it. I don't want to leave the shield down for long." She reached one hand towards the square stone panel embedded in the wood of the supporting column. "Ready?" she asked. I nodded, and she slapped the panel. I felt the shield fall, and used my natural speed to snatch the tiny stone fragment that I had my eye on. It took less than a second, and she slapped the panel again and re-enabled the shield. Surprise showed on her face. To her, I'd been a blur for an instant, returning to stand before her with a tiny piece of stone in my fingers. "Whoa...yeah, OK, I forgot that you Faerie are quick! What is that?"

I held it up between my thumb and forefinger so that she could see it. It looked like an animal tusk, which it mostly was, though it was made entirely of stone. "It's from one of them," I said, referring to the gargoyles. One of them had, indeed, broken a tooth when it had slammed into the barrier and it foolishly left the fragment behind. "Just how good a witch are you?"

A sly grin crawled across her pretty face, reminding me suddenly of the picture of her mother I had seen in the living room, and I had a suspicion as to the answer to that question before she opened her mouth.

"Yeah, I'm damned good. Give me that thing, I think I can get some information out of it."

I dropped the tusk into her upturned palm and she examined it for a moment. "Oh, yeah, I can definitely work with this," she muttered before turning away and heading for the kitchen. I followed. She turned a corner and faced a bookcase filled with cookbooks and various utensils. Keeping her eyes on the tusk in her hand, she absently reached up and moved a vase of flowers to one side so that she could reach a switch hidden behind it. There was a loud click from somewhere in the wall, and she moved the flowers back. Looking up from the tusk at last, she glanced quickly at me. "Don't touch anything in here, I don't know what might happen with your, you know...Faeriness." With one hand, she tugged mightily on the bookcase and it swung out away from the wall to reveal a darkened room behind it. She reached inside and flipped another switch and lights flickered on inside, illuminating a very witchy workshop.

Bookshelves covered the walls, and they were stuffed to the gills with books. Some of them looked like Amazon had just delivered them while others looked incredibly old, bound with worn leather and smelling of musty wood pulp. Tables lined three of the walls, and they were covered with neatly organized beakers, vials, papers, stones, knives, tools, and several things I could not readily identify. What looked like tilting glass candy jars were carefully arranged all the way around the room, filled with various plants, powders, liquids, and other substances, all carefully labeled in alphabetical order. It looked like a combination of a chef's kitchen, a pharmacist's shop, and a handyman's shed. An old wood stove squatted in another corner, with a modern microwave within easy reach and a sink on the opposite side. A computer setup with two large monitors took up one corner where two of the tables met, and it looked impressive enough to run the space program. The center of the room was empty, but it was easy to see why; there was a silver pentacle, a five-pointed star enclosed within a circle, plus two other concentric circles around it, embedded into the floor. Other arcane designs and carvings surrounded it, and I knew better than to step on any of them. The entire room buzzed with a low, constant hum of magick left behind from hundreds, if not thousands, of castings.

"This place has been in your family for a long time," I stated simply. Ariana had already pulled a small rolling chair from somewhere and sat at one of the tables as she examined the stone tusk. After a moment, she got up and pulled a handful of thick white candles from a drawer. Moving with practiced efficiency, she placed them at the points of the silver star inscribed in the floor and lit them with a long-stemmed fireplace lighter. Then she went to the wall and dimmed the electric lights in the room until they were only a faint brightness overhead, their wan light overpowered by flickering candles below.

"Yep. Built out here in the late 1830s, before Houston was even a thing. Had to start somewhere, and this apparently seemed like a good place. Ley lines, and all." She pulled a mortar and pestle out of a cabinet and began to add powders and herbs from several different jars. When she was satisfied with the contents of the small porcelain bowl, she took the pestle to it and carefully began to grind the mixture. She quietly murmured some words that I didn't catch, but I felt the tingle of magick as her spell came to life.

I was surprised by the power of it. After seeing the strength of the house shield, I shouldn't have been, but the potency of her spellcraft was high. I knew what she was going for, and I stood back and out of the way to give her room to work. She continued speaking in a low voice, her chant steady and strong. A warm glow began to emanate from the bowl as she worked.

Still chanting, she laid aside the pestle and stood, carrying the bowl carefully in both hands. She walked to the beautiful pentacle in the floor and placed the bowl just inside the innermost silver circle. Moving quickly, she stepped to another table and put a couple of pieces of charcoal into a small iron cauldron, then picked it up and placed it in the center of the pentagram. From yet another jar, she pulled a pinch of something and sprinkled that into the cauldron as well. She grabbed a long match, lit it, and applied it to the contents of the cauldron, setting them aflame with a strong scent of pine and wood.

Her quiet voice rose in volume and I felt the hairs on my arms stiffen in response to the power she had gathered. She snagged the stone gargoyle tusk from the table and placed it carefully on the pentagram in between the cauldron and the porcelain bowl of herbs, then she sat cross-legged just outside the silver circle at the bottom of the star. She raised her hands, palm up, as if waiting to receive something, and then she emphasized four words: "Me illis quae praecedunt!" She clapped her hands together at the last word, and there was a blinding flash, accompanied by a thunderclap that rattled all of the glass jars on the tables.

When my vision cleared, there was a roiling cloud in the middle of the room, centered over the pentagram in the floor. It was illuminated from within by a pale, shifting light. Ariana had begun chanting again, arms still held out to either side with her palms up. I knew that she was shaping the spell with her will, using the words to guide it into following her wishes. Spells were tricky things, and if your intent wasn't strong enough, they could go awry. It sucked when that happened, not in a good way.

The cloud responded to her words by smoothing out and brightening somewhat. When it had calmed, an image appeared on its gently rolling surface, like a movie projected on water. The front of the house which we now occupied was plainly visible, two figures frozen on the front steps. As the image became clearer, I could see that one was Ariana, still dressed in her blue clubbing attire, her hand about to slap the switch that enabled the house shield. I was the other, standing next to her in a defensive posture. I still never got used to seeing myself garbed as a human, my true form hidden by a strong Faerie glamour. Unless I deemed it necessary (or someone had far stronger mystical power than I), I appeared as an ordinary, nondescript human male, dressed in jeans, a simple collared shirt, and a light jacket. I noted that, in the stress of the moment, my eyes had been shining fiercely in the dim light of the porch. Gotta watch that in the future...can't have them give me away.

The image flickered and then began to move, and I saw the two of us turn our backs and begin moving away from the porch, as if someone had hit rewind on a movie. The porch dwindled in the distance, and I realized that I was seeing what the gargoyle had seen up to the point when it had slammed into the shield and its tooth had broken off. I had expected Ariana to be able to gain something from the tooth, for energy and memories could be carried in a piece of an organism the same way that DNA could be found in a severed finger, although they didn't stay viable for very long. But you had to be good to extract it. Damned good. I had expected her to possibly gain some impressions from it on the off chance that she could interpret them, but this spell was far beyond what I might have thought she could do.

The lights from the house continued to shrink as the gargoyle flew backwards along its path, back towards its origin. Soon we could see the highway below, a bright, gray river of light in a darkened land, tiny dots of color moving up and down its length, even at that late hour. It seemed to be heading back to town, towards the center of Houston, for it followed I-10 almost directly. Ariana sped up her chant, and the image followed her commands, the road flashing by at increasing speed.

More buildings passed below us, and the closer we got to downtown, the bigger and older they became.

A few moments later, the creature rose higher, then higher still. I recognized several of the buildings nearby and realized that the beast had flown straight from the heart of downtown. It was flying among the tallest skyscrapers, gliding on the air currents as easily as any bird. Ariana slowed her chant again and the vision slowed down to normal speed. The viewpoint of the gargoyle shifted slightly, rising a little more, then dropping to land on a balcony that overlooked the entire western side of the city. The eyes turned away from the horizon and I knew that we were about to see something important.

Just as the beast's gaze swiveled towards the interior of whatever penthouse suite owned the balcony, I heard Ariana stumble in her chant. The image rippled slightly, then the cloud began to churn and roll, making the picture unclear. The outline of a man's face appeared in the chaotic picture before me, and I stared intently at it, opening up my Faerie sight to the full. Eyes as green as emeralds but far colder, stared back at me. I felt a wave of darkness and hate wash over me as though I'd been hit with a bucket of ice water. Ariana struggled to keep up her chant through the interference, but fatigue was wearing on her. Before I could say anything, the shadowy silhouette made a flicking gesture straight at us with one hand. Ariana released an agonized cry and grabbed her head in both hands. There was an ominous thump, and a wave of power exploded outward from the center of the cloud she had conjured, and I threw up an arm to shield my eyes. It passed over me harmlessly and I lowered my arm to see the cloud dissipating. As it dissolved back into the nothingness from whence it came, it took the shadowy image of the man with it. But no matter, I had seen what I needed to see. I knew him now.

I stepped over to Ariana, who had fallen on her side, still clutching her head.

"Hey, you OK?" I knelt beside her and gently touched her arm. She groaned quietly, but answered soon enough.

"Ow. Yeah, I'm all right," she confirmed as she pushed herself slowly to her feet. "I wasn't expecting some asshole to throw feedback my way. That shit hurt!" Her tone was completely outraged. It made me smile. "That casting was supposed to be a simple retroactive viewing, just a recording of what Stoneface saw in the last half hour or so before his tooth broke off. I didn't think it was possible to ward against something like that, but apparently, that jerk found a way. Who the hell was that?"

She walked over and sat back down in her rolling chair. She rummaged around for a bit and found a battered old wooden box the size of a small suitcase. It had once been painted white and emblazoned with a red cross on the lid, but the colors had long since faded. She opened it up and pulled a very modern cold pack from somewhere within, popped the chemical bag inside it and smushed it around to get it going. This, she promptly placed on the back of her neck, eliciting a happy groan of relief. Her eyes turned back to me, and I could see that she was filled with questions.

"I know the guy. Elias Bress. He's bad news. Rich. Powerful. Donates large amounts of money to area hospitals, and then sends his guys to break the legs of the folks who owe him money. A real humanitarian. Cutthroat businessman by all accounts. I just didn't know that he had any magick to speak of."

She rolled her head a little, enjoying the coolness of the icepack on her neck. "Apparently, it's more than a little. I've never been hit like that through a spell, especially not through what was essentially a recording."

I thought about that for a moment. "There's a good chance that he doesn't know you were the one watching him. It could have been just a failsafe, a trap set for anyone who tried to see him."

She chewed on that for a bit. Finally, she shrugged her shoulders in resignation. "Could be. Either way, he's got to be behind all this. No way the gargoyles he sent and the creepy thug in the van are just a coincidence, they've got to be connected."

I nodded, remembering the dagger. An ordinary bad guy could have used any common knife to kill his victims, but this one had a dagger of summoning. Judging from that and from the Presence that had arrived not long after our encounter, there was something much bigger going on. If Elias Bress was a strong enough sorcerer to summon gargoyles to do his bidding, and be in league with whatever dark Presence we had heard, then it made sense that he was behind it all.

"But why?" I voiced my next thought aloud. "The guy's got money falling out of every orifice. Why would he need to kill a bunch of innocent young women?"

"Women? What women?" Ariana sat up straight in surprise. A note of fear and anger had crept into her voice before she could stop it. "Are you saying that the moose in the van killed others before trying for me?"

I turned to face her and saw her gasp as my full attention landed on her. I'm used to it. It's in the eyes, they tell me. My glamour doesn't hide everything. I looked away and felt her relief.

"Yes. There was a string of a dozen murders in town before I got called in. You were to be number thirteen." I recalled the scenes I had been given by the Goddess of some of the previous murders, none of which had been tidy enough for the evening news. There had been an awful lot of blood spilled at each one of those murders. Ariana would have been next. "With you being a witch and all, I'd say that's significant. The moose in the van is dead, but Elias Bress is behind all this, I'm sure of that."

"Well, if he's trying to pull something together that requires over a dozen sacrifices, we most certainly have to stop him! Whatever he's planning can't be good, and he needs to pay for what he did to all those other women!" I glanced back at her to see that her jaw was set and there was fire in her eyes. She was profoundly pissed off, not just for the attack on herself, but for all the harm done to a dozen innocents in the name of whatever kind of crazy goal Elias was trying to accomplish.

But I knew that now was not the time, and I said so. "You're right. We have to do something, but right now, you need to rest. You've been up for how long?"

She averted her eyes angrily, not wishing to acknowledge her exhaustion. The dawn was breaking, she had been awake for well over 24 hours, been knocked unconscious, thrown in a van and very nearly killed. In addition, the spell she had cast had robbed her of much of her remaining strength. She was running on fumes now.

"He's going to be too well-protected now that it's daylight. We'll hit him tonight, after we've rested and refueled. I have some things I need to do in the meantime, and then we can go together." I had no need of rest, at least, not yet. But she most certainly did, and I knew of a few things I could do to increase our chances that evening.

She shot me a look, her eyes narrowed in suspicion. "Don't think for one second that you can leave me out of it. I'll just find him on my own if you walk out on me now. I'm not about to let him get away with this." I could feel the weariness in her, but even more strongly, I could sense her determination, her powerful desire to have justice for women she hadn't even known about until just then. Ferocious, this one. With that kind of attitude, she might just survive what we were about to walk into.

I held up my hands in a calming gesture. "Hey, simmer down. I want him just as badly as you do. Whatever he's doing, he's tipping the scales, and I'm not down with that. Neither is my boss, so it's a done deal. It's my job to see that he's taken out. You're already involved, and you seem pretty damned capable, so yeah…you're in."

She sat back in her chair, a frown still on her face, but at least looking a bit more satisfied. "All right, then. Just so we're clear on that. You're not going to kick any asses without me. I've earned the right for some payback, here."

I nodded. She'd proven that she could be an asset already. Going against this kind of mystical power, I could use every possible advantage, so it would be foolish to leave her behind. After last night, she knew the risks. Hell, she was supposed to have died in a van last night, so every hour she lived beyond that was a bonus.

"Right. OK, go get some rest. I've got some work to do, but I'll be just outside for a while. I'll check on you this afternoon and we'll make plans for our attack."

Ariana raised an eyebrow. "Aaaand what are you going to be doing in my yard? You're not going to bring a bunch of Faerie creatures in my house, right? I mean, I'm just a witch, and I'm not the foremost authority on the Faerie, but from what I know, that sounds like a whole bunch of trouble to me."

I couldn't help but crack a smile. Had I brought some of my Faerie brethren here, a 'bunch of trouble' would be a vast understatement. I'd lived for centuries among humans. I'd learned to control myself so that I could blend in well enough to do my job, but I was a rarity. The others would likely make a shambles of her house and think nothing of it. "Yes, you're right. But I'm not bringing anything here, just making some preparations. Gathering information. That sort of thing."

"Ah, OK. Gotcha. Yeah, that's fine." Suddenly, her mouth opened impressively wide as she erupted into a giant yawn. "All right, I admit it, I'm beat. I'm ready to get some sleep. Wait a second, you'll need this before you go." She leaned off to one side, pulled a drawer open, and rummaged around in it with one hand for a moment before she found what she was looking for. "Ah, there it is. Here, put this on." Tired as she was, she still moved with a certain feline grace as she slid out of the chair and walked towards me. I could feel the magick from whatever she had in her hand as she approached, and I quickly stepped away with my palms raised defensively.

"Hey, now, wait a second. What is it?" My voice stopped her in her tracks.

She tilted her head to one side and sighed loudly. She was tired enough to be irritated, but too tired to fight about it. "It's just a stone on a leather string, Kane. It's a key to the house shield. If you're going outside, you'll need to wear it to pass in and out of the barrier if I'm asleep. That's not too dangerous for you, is it?"

She tossed the pendant at me and I snatched it out of the air, the intense tingle against my skin betraying its power. I opened my hand and found a small oval stone of the same granite that was embedded in the column on the porch. A small hole had been drilled through the top of it, and a leather lace had been run through it. From the feel of it, I could tell that it was exactly what she had said it was, and posed no threat to me. I slipped my head through the lace and let the stone rest next to my skin.

"Thanks. Get some rest, I'll be close by. I doubt anything can get in here, but if something happens, just call out. I'll hear."

She let out a dry chuckle and I heard the distinctive sound of a handgun's slide being racked back. When she turned around, she had a semi-automatic pistol in her hand.

"If some asshole gets past both you and the shield, the first thing you'll hear will be Bertha, here." She pulled a couple of loaded magazines out of the same drawer from which she had apparently grabbed the pistol and held them up so I could see. I could feel their presence from across the room. "My Mom made these bullets. Might work against magickal types, might not, I've never had a chance to test them." That sly grin slid across her face again. "Just be careful when you come to wake me, I don't want to have you be the one to find out how well they work." Without another word, she sauntered out of the room through the hidden door, leaving me with the beginnings of a smile on my face.

In my years, I'd run across my share of wimps and badasses, and folks that fell everywhere on the line in between. Ariana was way over on the badass end of the scale. Which was exactly what I needed. Sometimes, things work out a little better than we expect them to. At least, that's what I was thinking at the time. I should have known things would go to shit soon after that.

Chapter 6

I walked outside into the brightness of morning, leaving Ariana to get some rest. I could feel the buzz of the invisible shield around the house, and an answering vibration from the stone at my throat. Rather than immediately test its power, I simply stood there, taking in the beautiful day. The huge, wraparound porch was a throwback to a bygone era, though to me it didn't seem long ago at all. There was a slight breeze that carried the scent of the nearby woods, and I stayed still, gathering my thoughts.

This job had turned out to be far more than the usual slash and run. Granted, I was actually quite good at making dead bodies disappear, but occasionally, one of my kills needed to be left out as a deterrent. When the boss turned up gutted like a fish, it was far less likely that one of his flunkies would suddenly become ambitious and want to take his place. When I did my job right, that shit had always stopped right then and there. It was rare for me to come up against someone who actually had power enough to make me work this hard. Elias Bress was a heavyweight in the mundane world, rich and powerful and all that, but that meant nothing to me. Rich or poor, they all bled the same. However, it seemed that Bress also walked in my world, the world of magick. That suddenly made this particular game much more interesting.

I mean, there are creatures out there who could not only give me a real run for my money, like the gargoyles, but there are a few who could eat me for lunch and not need to burp afterwards. I didn't know if his power was such that he could call on them, but he was obviously no dabbler. If whatever he was doing required a dozen girls, a witch, and a dagger of summoning, then the stakes were pretty high. This was going to be dangerous.

I felt the grin crawl its way across my face before I could stop it. "Bring it on, Bress," I heard myself say. This was going to be fun.

Trusting in the stone Ariana had given me, I stepped off the porch and walked towards the nearest stand of trees. As I passed through the house shield, I felt its power wash over me as though I was walking through a strong waterfall, but the barrier didn't hinder me in the least. Good. One less thing for me to worry about.

I strode quickly to the tree line, thankful that the house rested on such a large wooded lot. I hadn't asked how much property her family had owned, but judging from the way her house seemed to be sitting on a huge island of forest while the city of Katy spread westward all around it, I guessed they owned a large chunk of real estate, and had for nearly two hundred years. It would be worth a fortune to developers, who would bulldoze it all down in a heartbeat to put those crackerbox mansions in neat rows all over it. For now, though, it still had a sense of wildness to it. Birds flitted among the branches, singing their songs without a care in the world. I could feel the other animals out there, too, though I had no need of them. Their range was far too limited for what I had in mind, and I needed a much higher order of intelligence for this task.

There was a faint path leading into the thickest part of the forest, and I followed it. The house disappeared in the distance behind me as I followed the trail that wound its way among the trees, and I opened myself to the magick of the forest. Small as it was, the wooded land yet held the power of the earth and nature, a bastion of the old world smack in the middle of the emptiness of modern civilization. I let my feet wander and listened to my heart until I felt what I was looking for, and I left the trail to follow the silent call. The grass, shrubs, and saplings were thick, but they slowed me not at all. I'd walked the forests primeval; this was nothing. A few heartbeats later, I found the spot, a rough circle of taller trees that felt like a shelter, a haven within the forest. I found a suitable spot and sat down, releasing the glamour that hid my true appearance as I did so. Sprites seldom appeared to humans, and though they could certainly see through my disguise, there was no need to confuse them.

Little ones, I beg your pardon, but I have need of you. Please help me. I spoke the words silently, with the intent of my whole heart. I was calm and polite, but insistent. Sprites are twitchy, but they also respect strength and control. Not every Faerie is able to find them. Repeating my call, I sat as still as I could, not wishing to spook any that came near.

Finally, I heard the faint tinkling of the tiniest of bells. I smiled. That jerk Disney got something right, I guess. I looked upward and saw three tiny spots of light drifting lightly on the breeze. One might think they were lightning bugs or other insects, and they often appeared that way as a disguise. I saw through all that, though. What drifted down to land on the ground in front of me on tiny bare feet were three warriors, each no more than three inches tall. Sunlight brought out the colors in their translucent wings, similar to those of dragonflies, though not nearly so long. The Sprites looked mostly human, though their eyes gleamed with intense power unexpected from such small beings. They were nude, their tiny humanoid bodies lithely muscled like the swimmers I had seen in the human Olympics. The leader was female, with a mane of red hair framing her upturned face. Her jaw was strong and thrust up at me, her expression imperious. She was beautiful in a way that only the Fae can be, regal and alluring at the same time. She was flanked by another female with dark hair and a male with hair of sandy blond. Both were stunning and aloof. Any human to see them this way, in their true guise, risked being unintentionally enchanted by them, obsessed with their comeliness.

The leader looked me up and down with an appraising glance before she finally spoke. Her words sounded in my mind, in a voice so beautiful that it would have made me ache had I been human. *You called politely, and we have come. What do you wish of us and what do you offer?*

I tried not to smile, for that might have shown disrespect. Sprites were far more powerful in numbers than they were ever given credit for, and although I'm pretty ferocious in my own right, it wouldn't do for me to find myself on their shit list. They had always been helpful to me, and to be honest, I liked them.

I must make war on a human in the big city nearby. I saw her face twist in disgust, and felt her disapproval. Hell, I felt the same about the city and all of its heartlessness and concrete, its unwashed masses, but I pressed on. *I would have your warriors go there and tell me what you can of his defenses. He uses magick, and may have fell creatures bound to his service.* She raised an eyebrow as she considered my words, then I added, *The Goddess has tasked me with this. He is tipping the scales. I mean to balance them.* Her eyes widened at that, and I felt her agreement before she spoke.

That is dire. We would aid you. What do you offer?

Fortunately, I knew all of the things that made the Sprites happy. *Silver. The dark fizzy drink. And a sweet.* She was a tough one, this Sprite, but she couldn't hide the widening of her eyes and the faint smile that followed soon after. For all their imperiousness, they had their vices. They loved the shine of silver, even tiny pieces, though they wore no ornamentation on their bodies. I had no idea what they used it for, but for as long as I'd known them, they'd been mad for the stuff. And none of them could resist modern sodas and chocolate. They couldn't get enough of it.

We have a bargain, Slayer. We will meet again in this place at sundown. Show me where the human resides.

I opened my mind to her and showed her what I had seen from Ariana's spell. I knew it was incomplete, but I guessed they could figure it out well enough from what I had seen. I added what else I knew about the downtown area, and I felt a sense of recognition from the leader. Whether she'd been there herself or some of her folk had been, I knew she had seen what she needed. Her lovely voice echoed in my head again.

We know of this place. We do not like it there, for it has an oily, dank feel. But a bargain has been struck. We will do our part. Sundown. She turned and nodded towards her companions, who immediately launched themselves upward, their lights disappearing into the sky like two bursts from a Roman candle. The leader drifted into the air at a more sedate pace. When she was level with my face, she turned and looked over one shapely shoulder, through the intense buzzing of her beautiful wings. *There is danger for us in this. Do not be miserly, Slayer.*

I inclined my head in agreement. To them, a full bottle of soda, a handful of silver, and a bag of foil-wrapped chocolate kisses would be a magnificent hoard. Easy enough to procure before sundown. She nodded, accepting my word that I wouldn't be a cheap bastard when it came time to pay up. They did not take kindly to such things. She held my gaze for a moment longer, as if strongly implying that she had her eye on me, and then she, too, burst into a bright spot of fire and flew off into the trees.

The birds had not stopped singing during our conversation, and they continued now. I was satisfied that the Sprites would come back with some good information, and now I had some time on my hands. The breeze caressed my skin and I allowed myself to enjoy the sensation for longer than usual. This was the calm before the storm, and although I generally prefer straight action, I could also appreciate moments of stillness. The morning was growing warmer, as is typical in Texas, and I enjoyed it. Minutes passed, and I decided it was time to get moving. I didn't need a lot of rest, but I could snatch a bit since it would be hours before it was time for us to move out.

I snorted at the thought. *Us.* I knew very little about Ariana, but now we seemed to be partners for the duration of this thing. As an assassin for the Light, I'd only worked with others a handful of times over the centuries, and less than that with humans. They hadn't survived when the shit went down. You'd think I'd be sad about that, but that's not how I roll, as they say. They knew the risks. Against my better judgement, I found myself hoping that Ariana might make it through. She sure as hell seemed to have some helpful skills. Maybe she'd make it. The thought pleased me, odd as I found that to be. I headed back to the house for what would serve as a nap for me. Soon enough, we'd see if either of us would make it out alive.

Chapter 7

I woke at the first creak of her foot on the stair. After making a quick trip to the nearest convenience store for the Sprite's bribes, I had lain back on one of the soft couches on the bottom floor and lost myself in old memories. It wasn't a true sleep, but it was close enough, and left me feeling very much as a human might have after a full night's rest. I sat up, already alert, as she emerged at the bottom of the staircase. Her hair was gathered in a ponytail that bounced behind her as she moved, and she was dressed in a pair of black cargo pants, a multi-pocketed tactical vest over a tight-fitting black shirt, and black cross trainers. She looked equally prepared to raid tombs or fight zombies. In my day, I'd done both.

"Stayed out of trouble, I hope?" Her voice held a hint of a smile in it. I found it far funnier than she knew since I had a much better idea of the trouble I could handily cause if I chose.

"More or less. It'll be dark soon, and we'll need to be on our way as soon as I hear from some of my friends."

"Friends?" Her voice rose slightly, laden with curiosity. "Are they of the Faerie, too?" She went into her kitchen and rummaged around in the fridge. She somehow assembled a decent meal in less than a minute and sat down at the table, already chewing something as she eyed me.

"They are," I confirmed. "They're skittish around humans, though. You might want to stay here while I go talk to them." I saw the dark look cross her face and knew then that she was going to make a stink if I didn't allow her to come with me. Not that I cared that much.

"Like hell," she said flatly. "That asshole, Bress, tried to have me killed. I'm all in here, and I won't be left behind like somebody's kid sister. I'm no lightweight, and you'll need me."

I turned to stare at her. I wasn't angry yet, but I don't take kindly to someone, especially a human, informing me of what they are or are not going to do. If I chose to enchant her, witch or not, I could have her thinking she was riding a unicorn in a field of poppies while I left her ass behind. My gaze locked onto hers and to her credit, she didn't look away. I did see her pale a bit, but she tipped her chin up at me and stayed firm.

She was tough, I had to admit. And she had saved my ass when the gargoyles attacked. She didn't even know me, but she had welcomed me into her home, which actually gave me a certain amount of power. As a witch, she had known that. I stared at her a few moments longer, then I shifted my sight so that I could read her aura. It still burned a bright cobalt blue, though I was shocked to see that it also had threads of gold here and there. I had somehow missed it before, and it is exceedingly rare, to say the least. That did it for me. Auras don't lie. The gold I'd seen in hers branded her as something special, even if I wasn't yet sure exactly what. I finally turned away and felt the tension leave her.

"All right, you have a point. I take it that you haven't met the Sprites before?"

She cocked her head to one side. "Sprites? What, like Tinkerbell?"

"They sometimes sound like her, but enough of them together could kick the shit out of her, the pirates, and all the Lost Boys at the same time, Peter Pan be damned. It's not wise to underestimate them." I frowned as I tried to figure out how to describe them to her. As powerful as she seemed to be, Ariana wasn't very knowledgeable about the Sprites and their abilities, their social structure. "As a human, you'll need to be very quiet, very polite, and you'll need to guard yourself against their, um...charms."

She mulled this over for a moment, then nodded. "OK," she agreed. "What little I know of you Faerie says that you're all, even the tiny ones, pretty powerful. I can respect that. I'll follow your lead."

I stood up and walked over to the table where I had deposited my grocery bags and picked them up. "I need a soup bowl and some thimbles if you have any. I asked them to do some scouting for me. They're good at that. This is their payment. It may be trifling to us, but they're dead serious about their bargains, no matter what the price. I was lucky they accepted."

She eyed the contents of the grocery bags dubiously, but nevertheless walked over to an armoire in the living room. She pulled out a couple of drawers and then found what she was looking for in a third. When she returned, she held out one hand in which three shiny thimbles rested. "Will these do?"

"Perfect," I replied. "Don't forget the soup bowl. It's almost sundown, and it's not good to be late for a meeting with the Sprites. Disrespect them and it could be centuries before one of them decides to speak to you again."

Her eyebrows shot up. "Whoa. Well, we can't have that. OK, hang on," she walked into the kitchen and pulled a bowl from a cupboard. She turned away, then went back and replaced it before moving to another cupboard and pulling out a different bowl, older and better made, with elegant swirls around the rim. She looked at me and shrugged. "Hey, if these Sprites are touchy, we'll want to use the good china."

The corner of my mouth twitched. I liked how she thought. Even if she wasn't that knowledgeable about the Faerie yet, she learned quickly. That would come in handy down the road.

"Good idea. Let's go see what they have to say." I turned to head out the door, but when I didn't hear her following, I looked over my shoulder to find that she had gone into the hidden room instead. She rummaged around in there and I heard some metallic sounds that I recognized as handguns being loaded. Moments later, she emerged from the darkened room and shoved the concealing cabinet back into place where it locked with a loud click. She now wore two small handguns in tactical holsters, one on each thigh. Her vest pockets seemed fuller than when she had gone into the room and I guessed that she had loaded up on ammunition as well. I started to tell her that guns don't often work against the Faerie, but then again, sometimes they did. And some of the bad guys would most certainly be human. Couldn't hurt to have some firepower along.

She must have guessed my line of thinking, for she patted the guns and said, "Hey, they make me feel better. I like to be prepared." She picked up the bowl and thimbles from the table and said, "Lead on, Kane. I'm all set."

I headed out the front door and down the porch steps, pausing briefly to look around before leaving the protection of the house shield. The day was easing into twilight, and what I could see of the sunset beyond the tops of the nearest trees looked to be a beautiful spread of orange and pink against the deepening blue of the sky. Birds and insects were singing their evening songs, and nothing seemed out of place. Satisfied that nothing was going to jump out and rip our heads off, I stepped through the barrier and headed into the woods where I had met with the Sprites earlier. Ariana followed closely, but remained quiet. She was watchful, though. I could see her carefully scanning the woods and the trees above. Good.

Soon enough, we found the small clearing and I put a finger to my lips, motioning for Ariana to stay silent. She nodded and waited calmly while I set the bowl carefully on the ground and the bag of candy next to it. I used one claw to slit open the bag so that the foil-wrapped chocolates would be easily accessible. I suddenly felt her curiosity swell; she could not see my claws beneath my glamour, and I'm sure she wondered how I ran my fingertip along the bag and it easily parted under my touch. There was a lot that she couldn't see under my glamour. That was probably for the best. Didn't want to scare her like that just yet.

I pulled out the soda and set it down next to the other stuff, keeping the thimbles in my hand. I would pour some of the fizzy drink into the bowl, letting them dip the thimbles in and drink their fill. Otherwise, I'd just make a mess, which the Sprites might find either amusing or disrespectful. I didn't want to take the chance; I'd hand them the thimbles when they arrived. Lastly, I pulled a handful of old silver coins from one pocket and placed them in a small pile next to the candies. Once all was arranged to my satisfaction, I motioned for Ariana to sit cross-legged beside me while I assumed the same position. I could practically feel her eagerness and anxiety, but I ignored it. As an assassin, I had learned centuries ago that waiting is an art form, a skill. I had honed it for a very long time, and I could wait patiently for hours upon hours if necessary. Ariana had no such training. I hoped that she wouldn't do anything stupid.

As it turns out, we didn't have long to wait. As twilight deepened, I heard the distinctive tinkling of tiny bells high above us. Ariana gasped at the sound of it and I quickly motioned for her to stay quiet.

Something was wrong.

The bells had been light and airy before, as I had always heard them. This time, their tone was darker. Slower. They sounded broken to me. Ariana's face was shining with delight, but then, she had never heard them before. I had, many times, and this was unusual. I scanned the treetops above us in search of the three lights I had seen earlier. Only two drifted down to the ground before us, and I heard Ariana gasp again, this time in shock, as they resolved into their physical selves.

The red-haired leader had obviously been through some trouble. She was dirty and tired, and I could see blood on her tiny body in several places. One side of her beautiful face seemed swollen, and I guessed that she might be sporting a black eye later. The male Sprite stood a step behind and to the leader's right, just as he had before. He was worse off than she was, bloodied and bruised, his face fixed in a stare that likely saw nothing. He held the third Sprite I had seen before. She hung limply in his arms while he stood there, numb and exhausted. Her dark hair dragged the ground, and I could see blood had flowed from a vicious head wound down into her raven tresses. She looked dead to me, though I couldn't be sure. Sprites are tough, no doubt, but this didn't look good.

The leader spoke up. Her voice was tired, but still proud. "We have done as you requested, Grim. And we have paid an unexpectedly high price for it." She gestured to the unmoving form in her companion's arms. "Larea was injured. She may live, or she may not. We will not know for a while yet."

I bowed my head in respect. They had known it might be dangerous, as had I, and they had taken the bargain despite the risks. Sometimes, bad shit happens. I barely knew these particular Sprites, but they were honorable and brave, and were hurt while they were acting on my behalf. Even though it was bad form to add to the bargain after the fact, I made a mental note that I would help the Sprites out for nothing if I ever got the chance.

"That is unfortunate," I replied carefully. "I am deeply sorry that happened."

The leader sniffed once, then haughtily raised her chin. "That is kind to say, Grim." She glanced over at her wounded companion and then stared at me for a moment, calculating. I could tell that she was trying hard to appear as though she didn't care, which told me that she actually cared quite a bit. She was taking a chance when she next spoke. "With your leave, I would send Marek to take her to our healers."

As two of the original parties involved in the bargain, both the male and the wounded female Sprite's presence were required unless I released them from it. It was well within my rights to make them stay, and they would hold no grudge, even if Larea died. Bargaining rules among the Faerie were extremely rigid; it was just how they rolled. I may be a black-hearted soldier for the Light, I may truly delight in some of the messier aspects of my job, but dark though it is, I do have a heart. I released them. "By all means, Lady. I hope she recovers."

Red-hair nodded to the male Sprite, and he wasted no time in launching himself into the air, a tiny firebolt speeding into the treetops as he carried the wounded one to a place of safety. "We thank you for your generosity. It will not be forgotten."

I watched the retreating spark disappear, then returned my gaze to the remaining Sprite. I hoped that whatever they discovered would be worth their sacrifice. "You and yours are most welcome Lady."

"You may call me Tatyana." She surprised me by giving me part of her name. I had apparently gained a measure of trust by allowing the release of Larea and Marek. I'd like to say that I planned that outcome, but I'm just not that good a tactician. And I'm a sucker for injured ladies, always have been. Dammit.

Tired though she was, the Sprite walked towards the items I had placed on the ground, her nude body still sensual and alluring despite her battered state. I twisted the top off the Coke and carefully poured some into the china bowl. Moving slowly, I pulled the thimbles out of my pocket and leaned forward to present them. She picked one, dipped it into the soda and took a long swig, then burped in a spectacularly unladylike fashion. Setting the thimble on the ground, she then reached into the opened bag with both hands and pulled out one of the Kisses. She deftly unwrapped the chocolate and then walked to a nearby stone, where she daintily sat down. The candy was enormous in her hands, but she took a massive bite of the chocolate and chewed thoughtfully as she looked up at me. In spite of the seriousness of the situation, I had to acknowledge that, three inches tall or not, she was stunningly gorgeous.

Between mouthfuls of chocolate, she spoke up so that we could hear her. "We easily found the tall structure you showed us. It was alive with wards, even in the bright of day. We penetrated the first of them easily, as they were simple. Beyond that, though, there were other defenses that were not as easy for us to bypass." She fell quiet for a moment, chewing.

"Will you show me? It will be quicker that way." I kept my voice as calm and reassuring as possible. Linking our minds again would tire her further, but the Sprites were durable little beings, and I knew that she'd be able to handle it. She had to want to do it, though. Like most of the Faerie, Sprites could be capricious.

She leaned back as she finished the chocolate, leaving artful smears of it on her beautiful face and breasts. I could hear Ariana's breath quickening behind me, and I knew that the little Sprite's raw sensuality was affecting her. Slowly and deliberately, the little red-haired creature licked her fingers clean. When she was satisfied, she raised an eyebrow at me, pondering.

"Yes. We will link as before, Grim. However, I assure you that you will not like what you see." A tired smile crept up one side of her mouth. "I do not envy you for what you must soon undertake."

I opened my mind to her and was assaulted by the force of the images she projected. And she was right. I didn't like what I saw, not one bit.

Chapter 8

The harsh light pierced his eyelids, bringing with it a kind of agony that he had thought couldn't exist. He groaned and threw an arm up over his eyes, but the light seemed to be coming from everywhere, and he could not block it out. Grunting with the exertion, he sat up and swung his feet over the side of the bare metal slab that served as a bunk. Pain throbbed in almost every muscle, and although he thought he had slept, he was exhausted. The days and nights had blurred, and he had no idea how long he had been locked away. His dark hair was long and unkempt, his short beard matted with blood. Most of his almost-naked body had been beaten, cut, burned, and pierced. Bones had been broken, and dried blood covered more of his skin than not.

He winced in pain as one hand drifted up to the thick metal collar that encircled his neck. His fingers drifted over the raised symbols that covered its surface, powerful spells that nullified his abilities, his very nature. The skin beneath the thick silver was bruised and bloody, and the heavy circlet had almost come to feel like a part of his own body. He had hated it at first, but as the beatings and torture had continued day after day, he had finally accepted it as simply another indignity to be endured.

He thought about standing up, pacing the room again, but even as he started to put weight on his feet, the dizziness and nausea hit him hard. A weak groan escaped his lips and he settled back onto the cot. The old feelings, frustration, anger, despair, they all threatened to overwhelm him. If he could just die, if he could just cease to be, then the pain, the bone-deep fear, would finally end. At times, he longed for that release. However, it had become painfully apparent that although they had the power to hurt him beyond anything he'd ever imagined, that blissful oblivion was denied him. Even they weren't strong enough to take his life, not like that. But there were worse things they could do, and they did them.

In his weaker moments, he had silently wept on his knees, wishing that the end would come, but it never did. Again, hopelessness filled him and he found himself thinking those same dark thoughts. He weakly clenched his fists in frustration as he admitted that there was no way he could do it, no way he could commit suicide so that he could leave his tortured body.

Then he took a deep, shuddering breath and let it out. A few heartbeats passed and he did it again. He allowed himself to feel all the hurts, to intimately know them without shying away. Once he had fully accepted every cut, every break, every throb of pain, then he moved past them. His mind reached beyond the roiling despair that filled him, moving deeper and deeper within. His breathing slowed further, and he sat motionless for several minutes. Finally, he found his space of stillness. The pain fell away, and he reveled in the simple absence of it.

From that place of strength, that unassailable bastion of calm and self that resided where none but he could go, he remembered who and what he was. Without realizing it, he sat up straighter and squared his shoulders, slowly assuming his usual posture in spite of the pain it caused. His unseeing eyes rose from the cold concrete floor and the tiny metal drain that was still clogged with his own blood, and his chin rose into its accustomed haughty position.

No matter what they did to his body, they could not truly touch him. He would never give them what they wanted, and try as they might, they could not take it from him. For a few moments, he became what he had once been.

The steel door slammed open, and two of Bress's thugs shambled in. Huge brutes, all muscle, sinew, shaved heads and tattoos, they stepped to either side of the doorway to allow Elias Bress to enter. He had left his suit jacket somewhere and was wearing a large plastic apron. He was putting on the second of a pair of black rubber gloves, which did not bode well. Behind him, a weaselly-looking little man with narrow-set eyes and receding gray hair pushed a metal cart laden with wicked-looking tools, knives, and pliers. He moved the cart to one side of the room, then began to put on a similar plastic apron. Bress glared balefully at him and the older man stopped, scowled, then folded it and put it back in a drawer on the cart. Bress snapped his fingers and pointed at the door, and the weaselly fellow quickly exited the room, resentment plain on his face.

When Elias Bress laid eyes on the man on the metal bunk, his eyebrows rose in surprise. This was not the beaten, nearly broken wretch he had left to rot on the floor of the cell yesterday in a pool of his own blood. This fellow sat regally as though the uncomfortable, hard slab was a throne. There was a faint tingle of power in the room, and Bress had the feeling that he had just entered the presence of a superior. The man's gaze finally turned to him, and Bress almost flinched at the calm power that radiated from his golden eyes.

Anger flared quickly in Elias Bress, and he stepped over and backhanded the silent man with one latex-gloved hand, knocking him off the cot and onto the hard floor in a jumbled heap. Bress shook his hand and flexed it as pain blossomed there.

"Don't you dare look at me like that, you filth! I own you! You're going to give me what I want sooner or later. You know what I'm willing to do, so you may as well give up now and save yourself some pain." Kneeling next to the prostrate man, he continued more softly, his voice silky with promise. "Look, I hate seeing you like this. Just give it to me and I'll kill you quickly. Just tell me where it is. I can be merciful, you know that."

The man on the floor slowly got to his hands and knees, then pushed himself to a cross-legged sitting position on the concrete. The same calm expression was on his face in spite of the new bruise already forming there. His golden eyes burned into those of Elias, making him stand up suddenly to escape their power. Bress recovered instantly, embarrassed that he had reacted with anything resembling fear.

The man's voice was raspy and deep, and it sounded as though it hurt badly for him to speak at all, but the authority in that voice was unmistakable. "Not a chance, Elias. Do as you will. We both know that you're not nearly strong enough. It's pathetic, really. Have at it."

Bress's rage was instantaneous and white hot. It was hours before he finally made the man scream, but he felt it was well worth the effort.

Chapter 9

"So let me get this straight," Ariana's voice was more excited than scared, and I figured that was in our favor. "Rich businessman Elias Bress is some kind of sorcerer, he's behind this rash of killings in town, and he wants to kill me, too. He's setting up something really bad, and he's got spells and goons and magickal creatures on his side. And he's holed up in a huge skyscraper in the middle of downtown Houston, surrounded by security and video surveillance, not to mention the cops he could call in. The odds are overwhelming, and we have to get in there and stop him before he does whatever it is that he's plotting. Is that right?"

Actually, she'd pretty much nailed it, and I said so. She actually surprised me by smiling. "That's AWESOME!" I raised an eyebrow at her. That was not quite what I had expected. Before I could say a word, she plowed right ahead, jabbing a finger at my chest for emphasis. "Look, I was raised to stand up for what's right, and this guy definitely sounds like he needs to be taken down a peg or two. Hell, he tried to have me killed! Let's go get this guy!" She walked over to the kitchen table, pulled both of her pistols from their holsters, and laid them on one of the placemats. She began to fieldstrip one of them, her fingers flying as she separated the pieces, looked them over, then began to put them back together again. When the first one was reassembled, she started on the other one.

I blinked a couple of times as I watched her. Her enthusiasm was encouraging, at least. And as much as I hated to admit it, I'd probably even need her help. The witches I'd known in the past had been formidable in a way that had been mostly lost over the centuries, but judging by how Ariana was tending to her firearms, I decided that she had something almost as good. It would have to be enough.

"Yes, he must be stopped. One thing to remember, though," I said. She stopped working on the second handgun and looked over her shoulder, waiting for me to continue. "He probably wants you dead because your death is part of whatever he's brewing up. I've got the dagger, at least, so he can't use it on you, but you need to stay alive anyway. Just in case your death will still help him somehow. It's what he wants. Understand?" I couldn't tell her that I had seen us together in the vision, that we had to do this as a team. I wished I had seen more, but even that brief glimpse was a gift.

Ariana shrugged and finished reassembling her weapon. "That was my plan all along, Kane. I'd just as soon keep breathing, and I don't give a shit what Elias wants. I'm perfectly happy to frustrate him in any way possible." As always, the weapons check had calmed her. She slid them back into her thigh holsters and turned to face me, folding her arms across her tactical vest. "So what now, Faerie? Are we going to head into town or what?"

I looked out the window to confirm that twilight had deepened towards night. It would take nearly an hour to drive to the Bress Building downtown, but I didn't want to get there too early. However, I had other concerns. "We shouldn't actually try to breach their defenses until well after nightfall. That said, we can't stay here too much longer. Bress knows where you live, and he knows I'm with you. Judging by what the goon in the van said before he offed himself, he knows at least a little of what I am, and that's more than enough to help him give us both a ton of trouble."

Ariana nodded thoughtfully. "Yeah, you've got a point there." She walked over to the fridge and opened the door. "OK, let's grab some food and then get out of here before some other creepy-crawly shows up. And I need to load up my backpack. Ten minutes?"

"Sounds good. We can head that way and stay in populated areas until it's time to hit the building. Do you have another car? Bress knows the little one, and we should use another. If the house is being watched, he'll see the switch anyway, but if not, then we've got a better chance of getting close undetected."

From deep in the refrigerator, her muffled voice emerged, and I could hear the smile on her face even though I couldn't see it. "Oh, yes I do. Ordinarily, I never get a chance to use it, but it'll be perfect for this."

"Good," I responded. Just then, a faint yet enticing aroma reached me from the open fridge. "Would you mind if I ate the pot roast you've got in there?"

She stopped rummaging and looked over at me. "How did you know? That's in a sealed container...oh, never mind. I'm sure it's a Faerie thing."

That made me smile. It's a good thing she couldn't see through my glamour. My fangs were out.

Chapter 10

Ariana's other car rolled along the freeway, its thick tires buzzing merrily on the pavement. It was a drab green jeep, outfitted as though someone had been truly concerned that a zombie apocalypse might be imminent. Roll bars, spotlights, reinforced doors and windows, a front winch, and thick steel bumpers on both ends made me think that someone had spent a lot of time watching *The Walking Dead*. I had the sense that it had other features, but saw no need to ask about them just yet.

"It belonged to my uncle," Ariana volunteered after several long minutes of silence. "He kind of had a macho-survival-prepper thing going on. Did a lot of shooting competitions and off-roading. Said he just liked to be prepared in case things went bad."

I let my eyes wander over the interior of the jeep, noting how clean and well-kept everything was. "It's in good shape. How did you end up with it?"

There were a couple of heartbeats before she responded. "He died last year. He was in Colorado. I never heard exactly what he was up to out there, but we got word that he had passed away suddenly. A couple of weeks later, a delivery guy drove this up to our house, saying that my uncle had left it to us in his will. There was some other stuff, but Mom took care of that. I took over the jeep."

Interesting. Her family certainly seemed to be possessed of skills, both many and varied. I made a mental note to ask her more about them later.

"Sorry about your uncle, but the jeep might come in pretty handy," I commented. It might have been a bit conspicuous anywhere else simply because of the additional modifications, but this was Texas. Extra-macho trucks and jeeps were everywhere, and most were armed to the teeth courtesy of the ubiquitous gun shows that occurred every couple of weeks in Houston. It would likely only get admiring glances from any human security that Bress might have watching for us until they realized that we meant business.

Ariana replied, "Thanks. I always thought it was overkill, but after what they already threw at us last night, I'm glad we've got the thing."

I had to agree. My plan didn't involve actually driving it headlong into the building while under full assault by the guards, but in my line of work, you had to consider all the options, even the messier ones. I was hoping we could get in, kill Bress, and then get out again as quickly as possible. At the thought, I nearly laughed out loud. Most of my incursions turned out that way, but that was because I only had to go up against humans. Not a problem. But Bress was something more. Not only was he a sorcerer, he had somehow drafted magickal creatures into his service as well. The gargoyles were only the tip of the iceberg, according to the Sprites. No, this was definitely going to be messy.

We took I-10 to the 610 Loop and went south to Westheimer, where we exited and turned east. We could have traveled straight into downtown on the freeway, but then we'd just have to wait. Easier to just make our way there as if we were out for a leisurely evening drive. We passed through the River Oaks district and slowly made our way towards the lofty skyscrapers in the distance. The traffic of early evening was busy, but not too much so, and I began to go over different approaches to decide the best way to get inside the Bress Building.

"The Sprites said that the building was warded. What can you do about that? Can you get us in without alerting them?" I could cover us both with a glamour or a veil that would hide us from physical eyes, but if I so much as bumped into a magickal ward, the caster would instantly know it. Ordinarily, I wouldn't care. I'd just bull my way in, kill anyone that tried to stop me, and then pull out the bad guy's heart. Hey, it's a living. But with Ariana along, I had to at least try to be stealthier. And the Goddess had shown me that she had to come along. I had no choice but to find a different plan.

"What, the fact that my entire home was warded well enough to keep out gargoyles isn't enough to tell you that I know wards?" Her voice held a chiding note that I didn't care for.

"I'd rather know exactly what your capabilities are so that I can count on them, rather than guessing wrong about your skill level when we're under fire. If you screw up, you might get killed, and that would only help Bress, which makes my job harder." Although I appreciated her help, I'd been doing this sort of thing solo for centuries. I'd have no problem cutting her loose if I thought she would be any kind of hindrance, and I'd do it in a heartbeat.

You don't live as long as I have in this line of work by being overly polite.

She was stung by my reply. That was fine with me. I needed her to remember that this was not playtime. When she did speak, her voice was tense with anger, but a note of apology was also woven in. "Thanks to my mother, I'm the best with wards that you'll find in this state. At least, the best I know of." She cut her eyes to me briefly and a determined smirk slowly appeared there. "I may not be strong enough to make freakin' gargoyles do my dirty work, but he's not going to be able to keep me out if I really want to get in, Kane." She turned her eyes back to the road, and the smirk became more pronounced. "And I've got some other tricks up my sleeve that'll help a lot. You'll see."

"All right then. My guess is that the wards are pretty close to the actual building. It takes a lot of energy to maintain something like that, so they'll want to be efficient. I'd say its borders will stay pretty close to the building itself."

Ariana nodded slightly, keeping her eyes forward. "Once I get close enough, then I'll know what I'm dealing with. If they're smart, they'll have a secondary ward just far enough inside the first one that intruders will think they're home free when they hit it."

I had to hand it to her, she was a smart one. That was encouraging. She continued, "If there's a sheltered spot, it'll make it easier. I can't imagine it would be that simple, though."

"We'll see when we get there. If nothing presents itself, I can cast a veil over you as long as you stand close to me. Once you get us past the wards, we'll have to play it by ear."

Eagerness crept back into her voice. "Right. Well, don't worry about me, I'll keep up."

I tried not to let my exasperation show. I didn't like this bodyguard business. She seemed capable enough, but knowing that Bress needed her dead was adding pressure to the situation. I couldn't just sprint ahead to get the job done, leaving her behind to get caught by his security team. One rent-a-cop's itchy trigger finger might be all Bress needed to cause Ariana's death and whatever big bad thing it might precipitate. Ah, well. We'd just have to hit it with everything we had and see how it turned out.

We slowly made our way closer to the Bress Building downtown, taking a circuitous route to pass the time. I looked out the window and watched the buildings, trees, and cars roll by. I caught glimpses of unsuspecting people as they strolled to or from their dinners, their amusements. They had no idea that supernatural beings walked among them, occasionally preying on them. Ignorance is bliss, I suppose.

Eventually, the buildings got taller, their tops scraping the benighted sky above. We rounded a corner, and the Bress Building rose up in front of us, all steel and emerald glass. "Cruise around the block. The Sprites showed me some, but I need to see it from down here." Ariana complied, driving as though she hadn't a care in the world, just another late night commuter heading home. In a zombie-proof Jeep.

The front doors were on the north side of the building, bracketed by granite pillars. I noted two rather beefy guards outside and another pair at a desk inside. The other sides had more simple entrances beyond stately trees in enormous planters. I found what I needed on the west side. A wide staircase led downwards to a lower entrance. A row of lights led the way below, and there were another two guards at the top of the stairs, but I could handle them. I'd have to be quick, but that wasn't a problem.

"That stairway looks like it might work," Ariana's voice was tinged with excitement. She had a good eye, too, it seemed.

"Indeed. Did you see that empty lot back there?" She nodded. "Go back there and park this thing. We'll have to approach on foot."

"That's a long way for us to have to run if we need to make a speedy getaway," she said as she turned a corner, heading back towards the tiny lot we had seen.

"Not for me. You have a spare key?"

"I do." She looked over at me briefly. "I never thought I'd be handing over my extra key to a Faerie."

"I doubt that we'll need to use it, but should we have to escape quickly, I can get to the car faster and come back for you."

"You know how to drive, I take it?"

I just stared at her.

"Hey, I just need to know what your capabilities are. Wouldn't want us to get killed because you couldn't drive us out of here...that would suck, you know?" She cut her eyes over at me again and I could see the twitch of a smile starting at the corner of her mouth. No wilting flower, this one. She gave as good as she got. I finally cracked a smile to show that I got the joke.

"Yes, I've had ample time to learn how to drive your machines. I just don't like them. I'm no Mario Andretti, but I manage."

"Who's that?" she asked. I just shook my head. Sometimes I forget how short-lived the humans are.

"Never mind. Here, pull in behind that vehicle, but face out." I pointed at an old suburban parked in one of the middle spaces. The lot was nestled in between a pair of older buildings, and could be exited on either side, so that was helpful. The bigger car would momentarily shield us from any pursuit that came from the Bress Building if we had to make a quick getaway.

Ariana drove into the lot and smoothly reversed it into the parking space. She put it in park and shut the engine down. After the long ride, the quiet inside the Jeep was staggering. Her breathing had quickened as her eagerness and anxiety wrestled with each other for dominance. I could tell that she was enjoying this.

"It's late enough, now," I began. "We can enter at that stairwell. I'll take care of the guards and then you'll need to get us through the wards.

How close do you need to be to tell exactly where they are?"

She pulled the keys out of the ignition, wiggled the spare off of the ring, and handed it to me with a grimace. "Pretty close, I'm afraid. As long as we don't move too fast, I can feel it before we hit it. Once I get close to it, then I can probably figure out a way to get us through."

"How long will that take?"

She shrugged. "Maybe a minute or two. If I can't do it in that time, then I can't do it."

"All right then. Let's go."

We got out of the jeep, and she went around to the back and pulled out a streamlined black backpack. She slipped her arms into its straps and tightened them so that it wouldn't jostle around if she had to run. It fit her body closely, and appeared to be about half full. Half full of what, I had no idea. She checked her guns and her vest one more time to be sure that everything was in place, then she jumped up and down a couple of times before shaking her arms and hands to loosen them up. Finally, she stopped wiggling around and looked at me.

"You're ready now?" I asked.

Though her heart was nearly beating through her chest, her eyes were clear and focused. "Ready, Kane. Let's get this done."

Chapter 11

Elias Bress knelt on a small, black rug, the smell of burning incense strong in his nostrils. The room was dark, lit only by a handful of red candles at the corner of the five pointed star inscribed in gold in the marble floor. The pentagram was deeply grooved and discolored, the yellow metal showing through old brown stains where blood had once flowed thick and scarlet. The star was surrounded by three concentric circles, and in between each were glyphs that seemed to writhe when looked upon. The symbols were ancient beyond any other written language, their meanings only known to a few still living, and to look directly upon them for too long meant madness. Bress had looked on them many times.

With careful, deliberate movements, Bress reached up and opened his robe, letting the shimmering silk fall in a pool around him. The air was warm on his naked skin, the parts of it he could still feel. His lithely muscled torso was entirely covered in thick scar tissue that mirrored the evil symbols on the floor. He had carved them all himself, some with the aid of a mirror and special blades that enabled him to reach his back. All had hurt him deeply, but the power he had gained in the process had been worth it.

He plucked a long knife from the floor near his right hand, his fingers recognizing the grip from long use. It was more ornate than the one he had given to Luther, but just as ancient. It seemed much heavier in the hand than it looked, as though it carried the weight of ages upon it, the residue of hundreds of lives it had painfully, slowly, taken over the centuries. With his left hand, he began the series of gestures that helped put him in the right frame of mind. Everything had to be right for him to call on those who empowered him. Words that should never have been spoken aloud began to fall from his murmuring lips and his spirit began to drift. Bress's surroundings began to fade as his soul floated towards a distant place, an eternally lightless, frozen abyss. Far away, in the deepest dark, slithering voices called to him. The ritual had begun.

As the point of the dagger pierced the skin of his chest, a bright scarlet light blossomed in Elias's mind. He gasped as his eyes flew open and his spirit slammed back into his body, an icy agony that stunned him with its intensity. He fell forward onto his hands, his stomach instantly convulsing. The dagger clattered to the marble floor, spinning just out of reach.

Elias retched horribly for a few moments, spewing the contents of his stomach onto the floor. When he had regained enough control of himself to shakily get to his feet, he picked up the dagger and staggered over to the wooden chest that usually housed it. With the ritual ruined, he needed it no longer. His hand shook as he carefully placed the blade into the velvet-covered bottom of the chest and closed the lid. Its warding spells flared instantly and he stepped away, slowly gaining strength with each breath. He slipped back into his robe and belted it tightly at his waist as anger finally rose in him. It passed quickly, though, and was soon replaced with a smug satisfaction.

One of the gargoyles had already alerted him to the girl's approach and the fact that the stranger was with her. The light wards that he had placed at the edge of the property were so subtle that even Ariana would not have detected them. In retrospect, he should have set the wards to alert one of his subordinates. He smiled and shook his head at the thought. He had never been one to leave the most important tasks to others if he could do them himself.

It was unfortunate they had arrived early, causing the alarm to sound when it had, keeping him from completing the minor power-raising ritual. But it was of no consequence. He was already strong enough to deal with them both. And once he had Ariana up on the black stone altar in his summoning chamber, he would complete the ritual that would grant him everything he'd ever imagined.

But time was running out. The heavens wouldn't wait, and the alignment would only be in place for a short while longer. Elias squared his shoulders and pressed the button on the wall that opened the sliding door to his office. Although time was short, he still felt confident. He had power enough, minions both mundane and magickal, and he knew exactly what to do.

He stepped through the doorway and back into his opulent, well-lit office, a stark contrast to the dark ceremonial chamber behind him. Without looking, he pushed the hidden button that closed the door behind him, then walked over to his desk. He leaned over and tapped a glass screen embedded in the flat surface. It came to life, elegant icons glowing softly, awaiting his touch. He tapped one, and instantly, a man's voice answered.

"Yes, Mr. Bress?"

"Collin, we have two guests arriving, one male, and one female. Please notify the goblins they have work to do."

A beat of silence prefaced Collin's response, which made Bress frown. "Yes, sir. Right away."

"Good. And Collin?"

"Yes, sir?"

"Be sure to lead them yourself. I want someone I can trust out there. Our guests are not unskilled. Do you understand?"

"Yes, sir!" The steel had resurfaced in Collin's voice. He would likely be dead within the hour, but there were others to replace him.

"Watch the southwestern entrance for them. The ramp. Let them get inside, then take them. Bring the girl to me alive. I don't care about the male, let the goblins have him. Carry on."

"I'm on it, sir!"

Bress released the button and walked over to a glossy refrigerator set in one wall and got a cold bottle of imported spring water. He drank it down and then disposed of the bottle before ambling towards the door to his private bedchamber with its bathroom and extensive wardrobe. In the event his guests made it past Collin, the goblins, and his other

96

surprises, he needed to be dressed properly to receive them. After all, he had an image to uphold.

Chapter 12

"Hold it," Ariana's voice was quiet, but urgent. We froze in place, sheltered somewhat by one of the huge trees that thrust upwards from planters in the sidewalk. I had cast a dimness over us both, though she had to remain practically within my shadow for it to work, and we had so far made it across the street to the Bress Building unnoticed. As far as we knew.

"What is it?" I hissed quietly, keeping an eye out for any of the building's guards.

"I felt something just now as we stepped onto the sidewalk."

"A ward?"

"Maybe. It was really faint, and I almost missed it, but I figure you need to know if I feel something, right?"

"Right," I whispered. I kept my eyes locked on the stairway entrance up ahead. The two guards posted there looked half-asleep, not alert at all. Suddenly, though, I had a very bad feeling about going down that way. If what she had felt was a ward, then he already knew we were coming. I looked around and spotted one of the smaller entrances on the side opposite the stairs and the main entrance. There was little cover, but it would have to do. "OK, listen, change of plans. When I say, just turn and walk normally towards the door on the north side, but stay close. I'm going to change the glamour so that we look like ordinary humans. But when we reach the door, I'll make us dim again.

That will give you the time to do what you need to do to get us in. Got it?"

"All set, just say the word."

"OK, go."

We left the relative shelter of the tree and nonchalantly made our way around to the other side of the building, looking to the rest of the world like a couple of ordinary people on their way home from work. Had anyone who saw us been asked what we had looked like, they would never have been able to come up with a decent description. Our images would just slide out of their memories, leaving almost no trace at all.

We passed no one on the way around the corner, although I realized that Bress almost certainly had cameras on us. I'd have to account for that. As we got closer to the service entrance, I gently grabbed Ariana by the arm and whispered in her ear, "Stop here."

I heard her gasp in surprise as a pair of nondescript figures separated from our bodies and kept moving forward in our place, walking steadily down the sidewalk as we would have had we not stopped. I saw her look down at her own body only to find it insubstantial and shadowy.

"It's OK, I've cast a veil to distract anyone who might be looking, but I can't hold it for long. Do you feel the ward here?" We turned our attention to the door and she went to work, pulling off her backpack as quietly as she could. She knelt a foot away from the door and unzipped a pocket of her pack and pulled out a tiny bag of what looked like sand. She pulled out a pinch of it and carefully replaced the bag. She repeated the process twice more, keeping the various substances in the palm of her left hand, and then she deftly slithered into the straps of her backpack again. Once it was in place, she said a few words, mashed the powders together in between her palms, and rubbed her hands briskly together. I felt her magick come alive. So far, so good.

She focused her attention on the air in front of her and placed her hands up, palms out, as if she were pressing them against a window. She said nothing for a few moments, then without looking at me, she spoke quietly.

"Yeah, I can feel it. I can see what the Sprites meant; it's simple, but strong. I can't shut it down, not without creating a serious disruption. Instead, I can create a small hole for us to get through that should leave us undetected." She looked up at me with an apologetic grin. "A really small hole. We'll have to squeeze through it one at a time. Give me a sec and I'll open it up."

I kept an eye out, but no thugs came racing around the corner to intercept us. Fortunately, no gargoyles came either.

Ariana began a quiet chant, words that I recognized from another time and another place which were very far from here. Her song was both a plea and a command, enticing the energy of the ward to open itself to us. She moved her hands in a circular motion against the unseen energy of the ward as she spoke, and I could feel her power building.

Her words finally halted and she made a curt gesture with her hands as though she were parting a curtain. Although there seemed to be nothing there, I could see that she was putting some muscle into the move. She grunted, "OK, quick...get inside while I hold it open!" She pressed her hands outward until they were about three feet apart. I wasted no time.

Being careful not to touch where I thought the edges of the ward would have to be, I quickly stepped in between her outstretched arms and insinuated myself through the invisible hole she had made. No alarms went off that I could detect, and she wiggled herself through right after me. Once inside, she gently urged the ward closed again, calmly asking it to heal itself and become whole, as though it had never been broken. She brought her hands carefully together and withdrew them from the ward.

"Whew!" She said, wiping imaginary sweat from her brow with a forearm. "OK, that was fun!"

"If you thought that was fun, prepare yourself. I think we're about to have a ton of it before long." I examined the door and gently tested the handle. Locked.

"I got it!" Before I could explain that I had a certain power over simple locks, she was working at it with a wire and lockpick. In seconds, I heard a click from within, and she grinned up at me. "Piece of cake!" Not bad.

I knew that my glamour would get us a long way, but they would likely still see the door open on some security screen somewhere. Not much to be done about that. We'd just have to move fast. With my hand on the door handle, I turned to Ariana.

"When I get this open, slip inside and find that second ward. Then we look for a way up. The stairwell here on the north side will be closer and less conspicuous than the elevators, so we need to find it. Ready?"

Her face was set with determination. She rubbed her hands together and replied, "Ready. Let's rock."

I opened the door and let her slip inside ahead of me before pulling the door shut behind us. Not a bad start.

Chapter 13

Slinging the assault rifle so that it rode along his back, Collin hurried along the corridor and spoke loudly, knowing the earpiece would pick up his words. "Reese. Kyle. Alpha says we have guests arriving at the ramp entrance. Have you seen anything?"

Instantly, a voice replied in his earpiece. "Negative, Collin. Street is clear."

Collin checked on the guards stationed just inside the entrance at the bottom of the stairs. "Rob. Carter. You guys good?"

"All good here, sir. Nothing to report."

Collin turned a corner and the smell hit him. He had hoped he'd get used to it, but that just had not happened. Goblins had a swampy, reptilian smell that rattled Collin to his core, but he knew better than to voice his disgust. Bress was counting on him. The goblins were his to command, and he was determined to make Bress proud. As he approached the huge double doors that led to the goblin domain, he turned his attention back to the voices in his ear.

"All right, everyone look nonchalant, but move to alert status. Alpha is sending me with the goblins. We'll be there in five minutes. If they show before that, keep them busy until we get there. Don't let them escape. Copy?"

Affirmative answers came back from both sets of guards. Collin put the other guards throughout the building on alert as a precaution, then turned his attention to the huge doors before him.

Unlike the other steel and glass doors throughout the entire building, the doors in this isolated wing were made of heavy timbers bound in iron, saturated with protective spells. Only a few of Bress's men had the keys to those portals, and Collin had them all. He took a large iron ring of keys from one pocket and shook out the proper one. The cold metal slowly warmed in his hand as he stared at the huge lock, gathering his courage to open it. Covering his mouth and nose with his sleeve, he took one last deep breath, and steeled himself for the stench he knew was coming. *Part of the job,* he reminded himself. *Mr. Bress is counting on me.* He slammed the key into the lock and turned it sharply, bringing a satisfying clunk from the mechanism as it sprang open. He stowed the keys back in his pocket, grabbed the huge circular door handles, and gave them a mighty pull. They swung open on a darkness so thick that Collin thought he could reach out and touch it. The smell made him take a step back, but then he stood firm against it. Low growls and snarls escaped from within. A pair of red eyes opened somewhere in the dark to regard him, followed by others.

"In the name of he who hath summoned thee, Elias Bress, I take command of thee for this undertaking. Follow me and obey!" Collin's voice only shook a little as he spoke the ritual words.

A ripple passed through the unseen crowd in the dark, and scores of crimson eyes opened on Collin. They would follow him. They were hungry.

Collin pulled the assault rifle around to the front of his body from where he'd slung it before and pulled the charging handle back to chamber a round. Somehow, that made him feel better.

"Let's move out!" Without looking to see if they followed, he turned and ran down the hall towards the southern stairwell. He wasn't fleeing them, he told himself. He was leading them. Yes, leading them. When he heard the thumping of their heavy feet, their deep growls and hungry grunts as they fell in behind him, he could not suppress the shudder that ran rampant down his unprotected back.

Chapter 14

I had to admit, the witch was pulling her weight so far. If not for the vision from the Goddess, I might have conked Ariana on the head, tied her to a chair in her house, and left her there, safe and sound, while I took care of Bress alone. Even so, I knew bringing her was running a risk. If Bress wanted her for his ritual, then common sense dictated that the farther she stayed from him, the better. But the vision had been clear; we had to do this together. And so far, she'd held up her end better than quite a few so-called tough guys that had taken up arms with me over the centuries. The only thing I could do was plow ahead, and that's exactly what I would do.

It had only taken a few seconds for a guard to come and check the door that we'd entered, but rather than gut him like a fish on the spot, I hid us in the shadows behind a column while he checked the door. I was glad I'd locked it again once we made it inside. The guard rattled the handle, but finding it locked seemed to satisfy him. He whispered an all-clear into his wrist as he walked away, not knowing how close he had come to dying a very bloody death at my hands. The moment he disappeared around the corner, we slipped through the stairwell door.

She found the second ward in less than a minute once we were inside the stairwell, and spotted a third as we neared the second floor. We passed through them all without a hitch. We headed up the stairs under cover of my glamour, and I hoped that we could continue to have that kind of luck for a bit longer. As it turns out, that was a foolish hope. Honestly, I knew it at the time, but a certain amount of optimism is important in any undertaking.

We moved up the stairs as stealthily and quickly as we could, keeping our eyes and ears wide open for guards. As we hit the landing for the fifteenth floor, I heard a door slam open far above us. Urgent voices echoed from somewhere up above and a lot of boots started slamming down on the stairs. Trouble.

"Shit," I muttered as I thought of a way to keep us both from being caught in the next two minutes or less. The door leading to the fifteenth floor was right next to us, but it was locked, and required keycard access. I swore again as I realized we should have ganked a card from one of the guards below. That would have been risky, but quite handy at the moment. "How quickly can you get through a lock like that?" I whispered.

As if in answer, the light on the keypad beeped and turned green. I grabbed Ariana's arm and pulled her with me as I flattened myself against the wall beside the door. It opened to admit a young man in black tactical gear, his eyes glued to his phone. Dim as we were, he didn't see us as he passed, and he headed down the stairs. Thank the Goddess for small favors.

Taking advantage of the slowly closing door, I slipped in behind him, Ariana right on my heels. The door shut behind us, and we found ourselves in a short hallway that led to an open space. The walls looked plain and utilitarian, almost unfinished compared to the upscale decor I had expected.

"Quick! In here!" Ariana whispered beside me. She opened up a door nearby and stepped inside, nearly tripping over a mop bucket as she did so. I followed her in and we closed the door behind us.

Just then we heard a beep, then the door from the stairwell slammed open. There was a brief stamping of boots, then someone barked, "Clear!" and then they clomped out again. The stairwell door slammed shut and the hall outside our hiding place fell silent once more.

We waited briefly, and then Ariana's hand strayed towards the door handle. I grabbed her wrist before she could touch it. Light came through the crack under the door, just enough for her to see me hold a finger to my lips. She nodded in understanding. I looked at the closed door and *listened*. It's a Faerie talent, to hear things far beyond the range of normal human hearing. My ordinary hearing is already far better than a human's, but if I focus, it becomes something supernatural. I stilled my breathing and *listened* to the hallway, focusing on the area just outside our door.

I heard the heartbeat first. It was thumping along, healthy and strong, and somewhat excited. It wasn't far away, only a few feet, just enough to tell me that its owner was standing guard on our side of the stairwell door. He moved slightly, and I could hear his fingers moving over the assault rifle he held, the hurried breath that moved in and out of his lungs. Suddenly, he started talking to himself, and his murmured words intrigued me.

"I've got this. It's OK. Nothing here can touch me, I'm OK. I've got the band, I'm fine." He took a deep breath and let it out in a quiet hiss, trying desperately to calm himself. This guy wasn't excited; he was terrified. For a rent-a-thug, he sure seemed skittish.

I turned to Ariana and gently put a hand on her shoulder. She seemed to calm under my touch, which was good. As daintily as I could, I entered her mind just enough to speak to her.

They left a man to guard the door. I'll deal with him.

Instantly, her response came through, urgent and strong. *Don't kill him! He's just a dumb thug, don't kill him unless you have to!* If she'd been startled by my mental communication, she didn't show it at all, and instinctively responded the same way.

In the darkened closet, I knew that she could not see my face well, though I could see hers in great detail. I could see her concern, but she couldn't see the intense eye-rolling that her comment had caused. Still, her request did have some merit. Some magickal creatures were drawn to spilled blood, and the less of it I left lying around while we were still undetected, the better. If Bress had gargoyles as flunkies, then he likely had other, less savory types around, and it would be best to avoid them if possible.

All right, all right. Just wait here for a second. Relieved, she nodded as she moved away from me, allowing me room to move. In order to enter his mind, I needed to see him. My hand tightened on the doorknob and I dimmed until I was naught but a shadow among shadows. Fortunately, the knob was in good shape, and it turned silently. I eased the door open and peeked out through the crack.

There he was, a young guy dressed in black fatigues and a military style ball cap pulled down hard over his forehead. The clear coil of an earpiece snaked down into his clothing, and his hands were white-knuckled as they held his assault rifle at the ready in front of him. His eyes were focused on the other end of the hallway, struggling to see whatever might be there while constantly praying that he wouldn't.

I slowly pulled the door open farther, and at last, his eyes drifted towards the closet and widened. The rifle barrel instantly came up, and judging by the way it shook, he was close to shooting already.

With the gentlest touch, I entered his mind and calmed it. I quickly gave him the strong suggestion that everything was fine in the closet, no worries there. The rifle lowered and relief washed over his pale features. That's when I stepped out and gave him a nasty chop to the neck, sending him to la la land, as they say. I grabbed the rifle out of his hands as he fell so that it wouldn't make a huge clatter. Looking at the kid on the floor, I couldn't help but feel some disappointment. On any other mission, I'd have preferred to just rip his head off, but as I said...stealthy, not bloody, that was the goal right now. I knelt over his body and quietly set the rifle out of his reach. I searched the pouches on his utility belt and came up with a pair of handcuffs, several zip ties, as well as a can of intense pepper spray and a few other toys. There was an ID badge on his belt that looked like it might be helpful. There was a glint of silver at his wrist, and I slid his sleeve away so that I could see it better. A simple silver torque encircled his wrist, inscribed with symbols I didn't recognize. They did seem to ring a bell somewhere deep in my memory, but I couldn't place them right off.

That's when something grabbed me.

Claws dug into my back and shoulders, sending bright lances of pain into my system, and then I was yanked away from the man's body and thrown far down the hallway. I'm pretty sure I hit every single part of my anatomy on the floor at least once before I came to rest. I shook off the pain as best I could and scrabbled up to my feet, staring back towards the hulking figure that now took up most of the end of the hall.

The thing was huge, and had to hunch a bit to keep from hitting the ceiling. A ragged grey cloak covered most of its body, though I could see a pair of glowing green eyes glaring at me from deep inside its shadowy hood. Jutting from the arms of its filthy robe were greenish, muscular hands. The fingers were impossibly long, and tipped with sharp talons that I had already come to appreciate. I was just glad that it hadn't ripped me in half, as most trolls tend to do. This wasn't going to be easy. I wondered briefly why Bress would have a troll here. To protect something? What could be that important? The troll hissed, bringing my attention fully back to him. Maybe I could talk him down. We were both Faerie, after all.

Brother, I am not thine enemy. I seek another. What art thou called? Silence, followed by another angry hiss, were the only replies. Not good. I'd dealt with trolls before, and even they could usually be reasonable. This one wasn't talking. *I have no wish to harm thee. I bid thee, speak!*

In response, the troll burst into a run, reaching for me with his dagger-tipped hands. As he moved, his hood fell back and I instantly realized why the troll wasn't talking to me. He was dead.

Not wishing to join him on the far side of the veil, I dodged aside to avoid his grasp, and ended up behind him. The best plan was to separate his head from his body with my own claws. I'd have to jump on top of him, but you go where the job takes you. As I leaped into the air, the undead troll whirled faster than I thought possible and slammed a huge fist into my side, hurling me into the wall. The pain was blinding, so intense that it was almost sweet. It turned to fully face me, and I could do nothing but clutch my bashed ribs. I just needed a few moments to recover, but it didn't look like I was going to get them. The troll leaned over me, talons reaching.

Suddenly, the beast jerked as though it had been hit. It stood to its full height for a moment, then staggered to my left, revealing Ariana standing behind it. The beast tottered and then fell face-first to the floor, cracking the marble tiles beneath it with its enormous weight. Jutting from the back of its head was what looked like a wooden broomstick. I was full of questions at that moment.

Ariana walked over and held out her hand to help me up. Her face was bright with excitement. "Boy, I'm sure glad that worked! I know I could have shot him, but that would have brought the stormtroopers in here for sure. Is that a troll?"

I willed my ribs to start popping back into place, wincing as they did so. I could heal my wounds quickly, but it always hurt. "It is," I grunted. "An undead one. Dead for good now, though. What did you do?"

"Oh! I broke off the mop handle back there in the closet and smeared the sharp end with some stuff I brought with me," she pointed a thumb at her backpack. "Kind of a 'kills-everything' brew with some silver nitrate, garlic, wolfsbane, iocane powder, and holy water mixed in, among other things. Nasty stuff. Looks like it took care of Lumpy, here."

"Yeah, that it did." I moved over to the beast's head and examined it. It looked to have been dead for a while. Its glaring green eyes had dulled as true death had finally claimed it, and its mouth hung open. Amazingly, it made me sad. I'd dealt with trolls before and although I had killed my fair share of them, I'd found them to be an honorable people. They had their own culture, their own customs, however warlike they might have been. To see one of them used this way by Bress...well, it pissed me off. Royally. He had no right to use Faerie folk this way. Gargoyles were one thing; they had always been a mercenary bunch, but no troll would have come with him willingly. And this one hadn't either. Bress had killed him, bent him to his will, and left him here to guard this floor. Add necromancy to the list of Bress's crimes. Bad juju, for sure.

I stared down one hallway, then the other. They both curved away from us, so I couldn't see far, but I knew that something of interest had to be around here. Bress would have just left his stormtroopers or even plain old security here otherwise. Whatever warranted an undead troll was definitely worth checking out. The thought rang true to me, and I knew that we were on the right track. Bress would be dealt with, but not until we solved the riddle of what was on this floor.

Chapter 15

Even with my Faerie strength and Ariana's help, it was quite a job moving the now-truly-dead troll into the bathroom. I'd had time enough to heal, but the thing was heavy. Stuffing him into a stall just wasn't an option, so we leaned him against the back wall and shorted out the lights so that anyone looking in there wouldn't see him right away. There was no blood to clean up, so that helped. We trussed up the guard and left him in the supply closet, dosed with a little something from Ariana's handy backpack to keep him safely asleep for a few hours. She was like a walking witch's pharmacy, carrying vials, powders, and several trinkets that seemed pretty important, based on how carefully she situated them. If she was as good with her guns as she had been with her other tools, we might just get out alive. Ariana removed his earpiece and jammed it in place in her own ear, then carefully muted the microphone so that we wouldn't accidentally broadcast our presence. She also took the silver bracelet from the guard's wrist. "Hey, it looks important," she had said in explanation. I couldn't argue with that. She tucked it in one of the backpack's side pockets, along with his ID badge.

Now that all of that was settled, we needed to get moving again. I pulled her close and cast a glamour over us. Our outlines faded to nothing more than shadows, and we headed down one of the hallways. I found myself wishing that the Goddess would hit me with another one of her momentary news flashes. Ariana's spell and the Sprites' memories had shown me that Bress would be on the top floor. And here we were, not even half way there, but figuring out the bracelet would just have to wait. Moving as quickly as Ariana could manage, we made our way down the hall.

We passed simple yet elegant doors on the left and right, but nothing screamed for our attention until we arrived at a corner. The murmuring of low voices reached us, and we stopped, easing ourselves up against the wall behind a rather majestic potted fern. If anyone came around the corner just then, they'd likely miss our shadowy figures against the wall unless they stared directly at us.

The voices were odd, guttural. And they most certainly were not speaking the common tongue of the land.

I felt Ariana's finger gently poking me on the shoulder. *Yes?* I thought at her.

What in the hell is that? Around the corner? I could feel her excitement, laced with fear.

I slowly eased myself along the wall until I could peek around the corner to see what was there. I was not pleased at what I saw.

A few yards down the connecting hallway was a small group of creatures that I recognized from half a world away. Their faces were the stuff of human nightmares. Curling ram's horns dominated their heads, and their wide mouths were filled with fangs. Their skin was mottled grey and red, looking as though it had been turned inside out. All of them were tall and broad through the chest and shoulders, with slender arms and legs that seemed too long for their bodies. Their hands were elongated and tipped with vicious claws. Claws like those had cut deeply into my skin as recently as a century past, so I was closely acquainted with their keenness.

They were lesser demons, all. I knew their measure. I was a match for any three of them. Of course, there just had to be five of them, sharing a haunch of raw, unidentifiable meat. Their table manners had not improved since the last time I had seen their kind, though at least, they mostly kept the meat on a table provided for that purpose. I eased around just a little farther so that I could better survey their surroundings, and saw that there was a large door in one wall. It looked very much out of place in the ultra-modern building, a massive wood and iron affair that looked far older than anything that surrounded it. The air was fairly crackling with magick.

Lesser demons, I sent to Ariana. *Guards, it looks like. I'll bet there might be something interesting behind that door over there.*

There's a door? Great, but what's making those awful noises? It doesn't sound good.

I carefully put my hand on her shoulder and guided her past me so that she could see what I had seen. She barely suppressed her disgust as she saw the demons at their meal. I eased her away from the sight.

Ew. OK, those things are gross and scary. How do we do this?

I paused for a moment, reviewing our options. Lesser demons would be able to see through my glamour once they turned their attention directly on me, which they undoubtedly would when I started trying to kill them. I'd only have a couple of seconds of surprise.

These are lesser demons. They don't like bright lights, fire, or silver.

Do any of those things kill them?

In certain quantities, in certain weapons, yes, I clarified. *It could get pretty messy, though, and we're still trying to keep quiet. Have you heard anything on the earpiece?*

Nah, just general chatter. I think they've forgotten about our guy back there. They're all massing at the bottom of the ramp we were going to use.

I allowed myself a hint of a grin. *That's good for us. Right then, I'm going to dive in there and kill as many as I can. Hit them with whatever you've got.*

Give me a second. I felt her rummaging around her vest and then in the pockets of her cargo pants. Close as I was to her, I could hear her switching out a magazine in one of her handguns, then slowly screwing a silencer into the barrel. She clicked the safety off as quietly as she could, then spoke in my mind again. *OK. Hit 'em. I've got your back.*

I doubt bullets will take them down, I advised.

These might, she countered. *They're my Mom's.*

I had nothing to say to that. I'd just have to trust that she knew what she was doing, which so far, she had. I gathered my strength and stepped around the corner, eager to finally have something to sink my teeth into. Literally. I stayed dim until I hit the first one. Then, every bit of my energy shifted toward the goal of keeping me alive.

I slashed the throat of the nearest demon with my claws. Black blood sprayed from the wound and it died even as it crumpled to the floor. As it fell, I left a row of deep slashes along the chest of another demon as it jerked away from me. Damn, it was almost as fast as me. This was going to be a mess.

I twisted so that I could plant a vicious Sparta kick on the third one, and I heard a satisfying snap as my foot connected with its sternum, breaking it like a cracker. It still managed to rake its claws down my leg as it flew away from me, and that hurt. A lot. Two down, three to go.

I whirled to attack the next one, but I turned right into a huge, open-clawed slap that nearly took one of my eyes out. I tried to roll with it, but I still stumbled and went down to a knee as I tried to get my bearings. Fortunately, I knew their ways, and I rolled towards the creature just as it slammed one huge foot down where my head had just been. My claws lashed out and severed one of its hamstrings, causing it to shriek in agony as it fell. I wasted no time in grabbing its horns and giving its head a vicious twist. Its neck broke with a loud crack. Take *that*, you ugly bastard.

That's when the last two jumped on me. Shit.

Chapter 16

Ariana watched the shadowy form of Kane disappear around the corner, and took a deep, calming breath. From the moment they had met, she'd had the feeling that Kane could take care of himself, though she had never really seen a GrimFaerie at work. An instant later, she heard the unmistakable sounds of battle as Kane engaged the demons, and she knew that it was time for her to get involved. She stepped around the corner in a shooters stance, her finger on the trigger of her Glock, and when she saw what was going on, she froze in her tracks.

Blood, both black and red, was sprayed everywhere and smeared on the floor. A couple of the demons were down, but two of them were pinning Kane as he struggled mightily to be free of them, and a third was clawing its way back to its feet, clutching its chest in obvious agony.

In that instant, all of her fear vanished. She lined up the shots and took them. POP-POP. POP-POP-POP. She shot the first two demons in their misshapen heads, and one of them went limp on top of Kane. The other shook its head violently, disoriented, but still alive. It growled and turned to glare at her, dark blood spattering the side of its face. It coiled up and launched itself towards her, dagger-like claws extended, its gaping, fanged mouth open wide in anticipation of the taste of human flesh.

Arianna ducked and rolled to one side. She took a pair of deep gouges along her side from the demon's talons, but her tactical vest took most of the damage. She sucked her breath tightly through her teeth as the pain hit her, but she came up in a crouch, her pistol in position. The beast had skidded on the smooth tile floor, and as it struggled to turn towards her, she shot it three more times where she thought its heart would be if it had one. The creature jerked with each shot, then fell forward as her special bullets finally did their work. She did not wait to see if it got up, but immediately returned her attention to Kane, only to see him back on his feet as he battled the two remaining creatures.

Most of his glamour had faded, but his back was to her and she could not see his face. She was surprised to see that he moved with a grace that was unlike anything she had ever seen. It was beyond even that of a wild animal, smooth and fierce. Although he was so fast that he was little more than a blur, she caught sight for the first time of his hands, their bony claws exposed and covered in demon blood. His hair was dark and far longer than his usual disguise allowed, and though his face was in shadow, she thought she saw a bright gleam of fangs as he snarled his defiance at the demons.

They slashed viciously at each other, moving so fast that she could no longer shoot without possibly hitting Kane in the process. Frustrated, she knelt and placed her pistol on the floor, knowing it wouldn't fit in her holster. Moving quickly, she whipped off her backpack, unzipped it, and then rummaged around inside until she had what she wanted. Without missing a beat, she pulled out her prize, zipped the pack, and whipped it back into place on her body. She held the artifact in her right hand while the other began to trace out an intricate series of designs in the air. After a moment, the symbols became visible as a trail of burning cobalt blue energy that followed her fingers in their movement. She began to speak the words of the spell, awakening it and charging it with her own power. Struggling to focus on multiple things at once, she projected her thoughts outward.

Kane! she called to him in her mind. *On my signal, get the hell out of there!* There was no acknowledgement as he ducked and weaved and fought with the two demons. They angrily tried to take his head off at every turn. Bloody wounds had opened up on Kane's body in several places; he could not keep this up for much longer.

NOW! she yelled in her silent voice even as she drew her arm back to throw the artifact. He gave the two demons one last swipe with his claws, then dove out of their reach, exactly as she had hoped he would. She hurled the object directly at the creatures as they stepped forward to follow Kane, and it impacted on the first demon's chest, its contents spilling over them both. Suddenly, an intense blast of cold exploded over them, and the demons screamed in agony. A wave of arctic iciness burst from the spell, its power freezing the demons down to their very cells. The wave traveled outwards over their hideous bodies, coating every inch of their skin as it flowed over them. They tried to escape, but in only a few seconds, they were covered by a permanent layer of ice and frost. As quickly as the flash freeze had begun, it stopped, leaving the hallway in silence. Three demons lay dead on the floor, and two pale statues stood by, screaming silently forever.

Kane pushed himself to his feet, his glamour back in place. To Ariana, he again looked like the nondescript fellow that she could have seen at any gym or mall anywhere; forgettable and ordinary.

"That was..." he began. "Effective. What was it?"

Ariana carefully stepped in between the frozen creatures and stooped to pick up something. When she turned back to Kane, she had a small broken glass object in her hand, a shattered sphere with a wooden base.

"Snow globe!" She held it out for him to see, and sure enough, the remains of a tiny winter scene were visible inside the globe, its snow and liquid all drained away. "I souped it up a little, though. Glad it worked!"

Kane looked at her impassively, his face unsmiling as always. A corner of Ariana's mouth quirked up in a smug grin anyway. *Yeah, I'm a badass, that's right,* she thought. She could tell he was impressed...not that he'd show it.

Chapter 17

OK, I was impressed. Most of the witches I had dealt with in the last few centuries wouldn't have been able to generate the house shield that Ariana had, much less the intense cold spell that she had just pulled off. Don't get me wrong, a few of them had some major power in one area or another, but they tended to specialize. Ariana's snow globe and the ward work that she'd already shown me were vastly different in terms of spell mechanics. I was surprised that she was so versatile. No wonder Bress wanted her for whatever ritual he was planning...she was packing some major mojo.

"Nice," I offered. I took a moment to assess my injuries. Some of the gashes had been pretty deep, but I could feel my body already working to knit them closed. It hurt like hell, but then everything did, and I'm used to that. Satisfied that I would be all right, I tipped my chin towards the door the demons had been guarding. "That's a pretty sturdy door," I observed.

She looked at me, somewhat disappointed, I thought, but she got over it quickly enough. Ariana tossed the spent snow globe aside and quickly retrieved her pistol from where she had left it. She unscrewed the silencer and stowed it away in her vest as she holstered the firearm, then focused her attention on the door. She walked toward it, stepping carefully around the corpses of the dead demons so that she could get a better look. It was locked with a huge, old-school padlock. I looked at the wall opposite the door, and sure enough, a big iron key was hanging there. Ariana reached for the key, but I put out a hand to stop her.

Of course, I was inclined to release anything that Bress might have been holding captive, but experience had taught me that was not always the best idea. Whatever he had in there might just as easily eat us both for lunch.

"Hold on, let's see if we can sense anything behind the door. It could be dangerous."

"It could be a prisoner!" Ariana retorted urgently.

"Maybe. And it could be something that works for Bress, but needs to be caged between jobs. Something big with a lot of teeth."

That thought hadn't occurred to her. "Oh, yeah, that would be bad. OK, let me give it a shot."

We stepped up to the door. She sat down and slipped off her backpack again, reaching in and pulling out a candle and a few other tiny items that she set between herself and the door: a small magnifying glass, a detached earpiece from a set of earbud headphones, and a piece of sandpaper about the size of a thumbnail. She lit the candle and then sat cross-legged before the objects. She closed her eyes and began to murmur softly as she cast her spell.

I had seen enough to know that the items represented the senses she was trying to augment: sight, sound, and touch. The spell she was casting would increase all of those to supernatural levels, if only for a short time. Mine, however, were already working at that level. I edged closer to the door and laid my left hand on it, sending my senses beyond the hardened wood as I did so.

Nothing. Not a thing. It was as though the door was backed up to outer space. I had never felt anything quite like it, and that was disturbing. I am a being that was initially created from the very energy of life. I'm of the Faerie. I'm connected to everything in this world on a deep, fundamental level, and should have been able to sense *something* there, but it was a complete blank to me. I don't spook easily, but I felt the hairs on the back of my neck stand up at the vast sense of nothingness that confronted me from behind that door.

"OK, that's weird." Ariana's voice was quiet and perplexed.

"Nothing?" I half-hoped that she had managed to sense something.

"Nothing at all. It's dead as a doornail in there." Her eyes were unfocused as she reached out with her spirit, pushed forward by the magick she had cultivated. She stayed that way a few moments longer, her eyes glazed and distant, then she suddenly shook her head as if to clear it. She looked up at me, her expression puzzled. "What is it?"

I looked at the door again and tried to imagine what could be behind it. The key was right there on the wall behind us. I could open the door and we'd find out. And then again, I could open it and we'd be dead. I reached over and snatched the key off of the hook on the wall and handed it to her. She didn't take it right away.

"I don't know what's back there, but I'd feel better if we kept this key with us. Whatever it is, we might not want it to get out at all. I know some folks who can look into it after we're done here." I never enjoyed calling on the Higher Faerie; they were always on the snooty side. Sometimes, though, they had their uses. This felt like it might be on that level. The Wise Ones didn't like to be disturbed, but screw them. I held the key out to her, waiting.

She cocked her head at me in confusion, but finally took the key and stashed it away in her backpack. I remembered thinking that the pack was overkill for a short incursion, but it had come in handy already.

"Right. OK then, where to next?" She gathered up her trinkets and tucked them away in her backpack, then slipped her arms through its straps. "The stairwells are likely guarded by now. I don't like the idea of getting trapped in an elevator, either."

"He'll have cameras, if not everywhere, then certainly as we approach his floor. We'll have to use the elevator shafts to avoid detection," I said. We were already halfway to the top, and I could climb just fine, carrying her if I had to. It would be awkward, but doable. I could immediately see that she didn't like that idea.

"I've got a better idea. Use that glamour of yours to look like that guard back there and I'll act like your prisoner. Then we can just walk up, take out whatever guards are at the top, and bam! We're in! Besides, don't you have some kind of woo woo thing you can do to them? Enchant them so we can slip past? They're going to see us anyway at some point, we might as well save our energy."

I stared at her. Honestly, I'd been looking forward to the climb. Still, it would be much easier her way, and of course, I could glamour a few thugs. Certainly, it would be worth a try. If we ran into trouble, all we had to do was bully our way through the entrance to the nearest floor, bar the door, and we could regroup.

"All right then. We'll do that," I agreed. Her expression was absurdly smug. I just shook my head and led the way back towards the stairs.

Chapter 18

"You see those last UFC fights?"

The new guy was a blue belt in Brazilian Jiu Jitsu. Curt knew this because he would not...stop...talking about it. Curt tried not to roll his eyes and sighed instead. His own training had occurred mostly in the sands of Afghanistan with men who had taught him to kill opponents rather than make them tap out. Still, he did not want to be a jerk to the new kid, so he tried to make conversation.

"Lots of knockouts?"

"Yeah, man!" Brett crowed. "But I'd have just taken them to the ground. Nullifies their striking, you know. I'd have stopped that shit cold."

"Because you're a blue belt," Curt suggested.

"Almost purple!" Brett corrected. "Any day now, coach is gonna give me another stripe and then...hey, you hear that?"

A door had closed somewhere below them in the stairwell, and now footsteps echoed from the bare walls.

Both men shouldered their weapons instantly, and Curt gestured for Brett to stay back. The older man eased himself to the railing and carefully leaned over to take a look, one hand hovering over the mike pinned to his lapel.

"It's me," a voice drifted up from below. "All clear. Bringing someone up."

The voice sounded familiar, although Curt couldn't place it right away, and he relaxed. Turning to the wide-eyed Brett, he said, "It's all right. It's either Burns or Sammy." Brett sighed in relief and slung his rifle back over his shoulder.

Seconds later, one of their own reached the landing, his hat pulled down over his eyes. He was escorting a young blonde woman with her hands cuffed behind her back. Curt's eyes were instantly drawn to her, and once he got a better view, he couldn't look anywhere else. The clear blue of her eyes, the spun gold of her hair...she was gorgeous.

"Is that one of the two we're supposed to watch for?" Brett's eagerness was clear in his voice, high-pitched and wavering. "Holy shit, she's hot!"

Ordinarily, Curt would not have tolerated Brett's outburst, but he barely noticed it. All he could see was the girl. He was completely captivated.

"Hey, Loverboy," the girl purred. Curt's heart skipped a beat at the sound of it. He had never before seen anyone so painfully beautiful. Brett squeaked something in response behind him, but he ignored it.

"Ah," he stuttered, struggling to speak coherently.

"Taking her to Bress, as instructed," the guard mumbled. "No need to announce us, I'll have her there in just a minute. Everything's fine here. Act like you didn't even see us." He led the girl past Curt and Brett, and their eyes remained riveted on her. She blew them a kiss as she went by.

"No...need...to announce you. Right." Curt mumbled dreamily.

"Everything's fine here. Didn't even see you." Brett echoed in the same slurring tone.

The guard pulled his keycard out on its retractable cord and flashed it in front of the sensor at the door, turning its light from red to green. He opened the door and ushered the girl through before letting it shut quietly behind them.

Curt and Brett stared at the blank steel of the door for nearly a minute. Finally, Curt blinked his eyes a few times and turned around to look down the stairs again. He had been sure he had heard something. When nothing materialized out of the thin air of the stairwell, he shrugged and went back to standing on his side of the door they were guarding. He was glad nothing had been there.

Brett's voice suddenly piped up. "Yes sir, gonna get that stripe any day now, you wait and see. That one, and then two more, and then I'm a purple belt! I'm practically one now. I got a lapel choke on this guy the other night, you should have seen it..."

Curt sighed. It was going to be a long night.

Chapter 19

"Now, wasn't that easier than just killing them?" Ariana's smile was impressively smug.

"In a way, sure," I admitted. "However, now they're still there in case of alarm. We'll probably have to deal with them later anyway."

"True," Ariana answered. "But for now, they're still there, and they think nothing is wrong. It'll be confusing for those guys at the very least. And there's no bloody mess of body parts to alert anyone otherwise."

She had a point there. Although I preferred to leave a lot more dead bad guys in my wake, stealth was getting us pretty far in this mission, and the sheer number of enemies in the building meant it was going to take more than my usual level of caution. "All right, yes. It was a great idea," I offered. She beamed. "Now, let's get on with it."

Whereas the floors below were more utilitarian, this floor was far more plush and opulent. Framed artwork on the walls looked like originals to me, though I was no connoisseur. I had simply been around when some of them were painted and recognized the style. A hallway with soft leather couches along its length led to an empty reception desk. On either side of the desk were large glass doors, frosted to obscure the view. They looked important.

"No guard?" Ariana whispered, puzzled.

Just then my heightened senses picked up the faint sound of a urinal flushing. I craned my neck to see there were bathrooms on either side of the reception desk. I gestured for Ariana to step behind a tall potted plant while I moved up beside the door to the men's room, dimming myself as I went. The door to the bathroom opened and a burly man in a suit emerged. He straightened his tie and moved smoothly behind the desk, checking two big monitors carefully as he settled himself into the chair. After scanning the screens, he touched his earpiece and spoke. "Ground Floor, this is Gatekeeper. All clear on twenty-nine. Alpha still in residence in the penthouse. Any sign of Jack and Jill?"

The response in his earpiece was harder to hear, but I could still make it out. "Negative. All eyes open, over." There was a pause, then, "Any chance it's a goose chase, 'Keep?"

"Negative, Ground. Alpha says Priority One. Goblins headed your way for level one support. Should have been there by now."

The pause was longer this time, and the reply held hints of both disgust and resignation. "Copy that, 'Keep. They've been here a while. We're in position and awaiting first contact. Out."

The man who called himself the Gatekeeper nodded slightly, then pulled a gun from beneath his jacket and ejected the magazine. After checking to see that it was fully loaded, he reseated it in the gun, racked the slide, then carefully laid the weapon on the desk in front of him. He then slid open a drawer on his left and pulled out a short-barreled AR style rifle with a round drum magazine. He checked its ammo as well, snapped the charging handle back to chamber a round, then placed the rifle under his desk within easy reach. Reassured that he was prepared for whatever might assail him, the Gatekeeper went back to checking the monitors, a dutiful employee at work. A good soldier.

I felt my claws extending through the skin of my fingertips, then with some effort, I pulled them back in. The guy was just doing his job. He'd kill me given half a chance, but only because he was being paid. He wasn't like Bress. He wasn't...evil. I debated for a moment longer, weighing the benefits of spraying his blood on the wall and moving forward, and then I got an idea. Maybe he could be useful.

Keeping myself dim, I moved silently around the desk next to him so that I could see the screens he was constantly scanning. Focused as he was on the monitors, he didn't notice me at all. Gently, I eased into his mind with my magick.

His mind was simple, but orderly. Although not the sharpest tool in the shed, the man had a strong work ethic and a desire for organization that had obviously worked in his favor. I probed a bit deeper and found that he was also a cold and hard man. Had no family and wanted none. And would definitely kick a puppy, but only if paid well to do it. I let my claws slip again. I liked puppies.

Reining in my temper and my claws, I sent the suggestion that he should relax, that everything was all right and there was no need for alarm. His shoulders sagged a bit and I heard him sigh as the tension left his body. Then I wrapped my arm around his neck and strangled him until he passed out. I arranged his arms on the desk and leaned his head over onto them. The blood flow to his brain would return in seconds, waking him, but my magick gently soothed him into a deeper sleep that would last a few minutes longer. I left him snoozing with the suggestion that he had only nodded off for a moment, and that all was well.

Ariana left her place behind the potted plant and joined me behind the desk. She scanned the screens and then leaned over and opened the drawers to the desk. In one of the top drawers, she found a laminated card that showed the layout of the floor and she got excited.

"Look!" she exclaimed. She pointed to a spot on the card. "We're here. We can get past these doors with his ID card, and we're only one floor down from Bress!"

I looked over her shoulder and embedded the layout in my mind. I touched another spot on the map. "There's a private elevator here. We can slip in here and then," I turned to grin at her, "climb up the shaft."

Her frown was intensely amusing to me just then.

"What is it with you and climbing elevator shafts?"

Still grinning, I shook my head. "It's not that I like it. It's just the easiest way up that won't instantly alert anyone. We can jimmy open the door and be on the floor above without the moving elevator showing up on anyone's computer. Besides," I winked at her, "it's still easier than going up on the outside. I've done that before, too, and it's far more difficult. For a human, I mean."

Ariana sighed, then brightened as she pointed to another spot on the card in her hand. "Look, there are three stairwells leading up. These two on the outside go all the way to the ground floor, and we came up this one here, but I think the one in the middle only leads to the floor above us. Let's at least try that one first."

I looked at the card and saw what she meant. Since it was an interior staircase, inside the usual perimeter of guards, there was a chance no one would be stationed there. And, to my disappointment, it would be much easier than the shaft. "All right, have it your way. Let's check it out."

I grabbed the sleeping guard's ID card. He looked like a higher level flunkie. The other card might have made someone suspicious when it turned up on a scanner on this level. As an afterthought, I replaced the card I took with the previous one. He would likely not notice the difference right away. Anything that might give us a few more minutes before they sounded an alarm was worthwhile to my way of thinking.

A quick swipe at the panel next to the leftmost door turned the indicator green and we were through. The lights were low, but it was easy enough to see we were in a plushly furnished waiting area that looked big enough to play tennis in. Stately-looking offices and other wooden doors lined one wall, and windows looked out over the city on the other. Everything was old wood and leather, and the smells were a welcome change from the sterile chambers we had passed through. Across from where we had come in was another set of double doors, made of wood instead of frosted glass. They were heavy and thick, obviously made with old school security in mind. If they had a locking bar on the far side, it would be nearly impossible for most intruders to get through. I grinned. I could get through them, given enough time.

I took another deep breath and stopped dead in my tracks. Somewhere underneath the leather and furniture polish, there was a faint, reptilian smell that set my teeth on edge. Most humans wouldn't recognize it, but it put my hackles up immediately. It smelled like goblin spoor to me.

"Whoa. Something's bad here. Goblins?" Ariana murmured next to me, and I raised an eyebrow. Apparently, she had recognized it too. My estimation of her skills went up another notch. Just then, there was a muffled sound behind one of the nearby doors as something bumped into it from the other side.

"Quick," I whispered, "get behind that chair and..." I looked and she was already gone. I had no idea where. I turned my attention back to the room, searching for an enemy to fight, all too aware that any commotion might still wake the goon at the reception desk. I crouched, dimmed myself, and crept over to the right side of the room, near the offices. Keeping my eyes open and my shoulder to the wall, I moved slowly forward as I tried to identify the threat.

I crouched, ready to spring if the need arose. The rattling door opened, and an older man in a lab coat backed into the room. He looked somewhat frail, with stick-like arms and legs that reminded me of a scarecrow. He had thinning gray hair and a face that resembled nothing so much as a rodent. He was pulling what looked like a medical cart, stainless steel with large, rubber wheels. Various surgical implements lay on its cold, metal surface, gleaming redly in the dim light. As he moved, I saw that he had smears of crimson on his sleeves. The coppery tang of blood made my mouth water just a little, and a swallowed the sensation away as I kept eyes on the man. He mumbled to himself and kept his gaze downcast as he pulled the cart through the doorway. Once he was clear, he let the door slowly begin to swing shut as he oriented the cart in the direction he was headed.

I thought about killing him, but then figured letting him go might not be a bad idea. If we disrupted the routine on this floor, they would instantly spring to the defense. If we let things move along, then we'd have the element of surprise on our side. As much as I generally love wet work, we'd been successful in keeping attention from ourselves, and it had worked out so far. Stealthy was good. Maybe Ariana was rubbing off on me.

Just then I caught a glimpse of Ariana, and wondered if it was the other way around. She had silently crawled behind one of the couches nearest the coated man and was apparently about to attack him.

No, no! I yelled into her mind. *Let him go!*

My command caught her just as she was about to pounce, and she stopped herself. She nudged the couch with her elbow, though. The man with the cart squeaked in fear and stopped suddenly. With shaking hands, he pulled a gun from inside his coat and whirled to face the empty room. I could feel his heart stuttering in his chest as fear raced through him, but the look on his face had hardened in spite of his fear. He scanned the room carefully before finally putting the gun away and shaking his head in disgust at himself. With a shuddering sigh, he turned back to his cart and pushed it away from the door he had just left and toward the big double doors.

"Damn it," he muttered, "Now I'm hearing things that aren't there! Need a vacation. A long one. See how Bress likes it with me gone. Treats me like a lackey, but he'll not get anything out of him without me...amateur!" He continued mumbling to himself as he pulled one of the big oak doors open, revealing a hallway beyond. He rolled the cart through and the heavy door closed behind him as he headed down the hall. The door he had used to enter the room was still slowly swinging shut.

As I watched the smaller door close, a flash of intuition struck me, and hard. I bolted forward and grabbed the door so that it wouldn't close all the way.

"Hey," I said quietly. "We need to go in here." Ariana stood and walked over to me, keeping her eyes on the hallway that had just swallowed the complaining doctor. When she turned to me, I could already see the questions forming. "Just follow me. I know what I'm doing." I paused. "More or less," I added. She rolled her eyes slightly, but said nothing as she moved to follow my lead. "And what was that, going to attack the guy? I'm the one who wants to attack everything, not you!"

"I don't know, something about him upset me," she answered somewhat sheepishly. "Won't happen again."

"Fine," I answered. "Let's keep moving, I need to check something."

The hallway was less fancy than the room we had left, though still paneled in wood. It led away from us and then branched in either direction up ahead. I sensed nothing approaching, but prepared for the worst, just in case. As we approached the end of the hallway, I felt a strong pull to my left, so I followed it. The wood paneling gave way to what looked like stainless steel, with doors evenly spaced along both sides of the hallway. Each had a keypad on the wall beside it, as well as a small, shuttered window at eye-level. A strong smell of blood and human waste lingered on the air.

"What is this?" Ariana asked quietly.

"This is definitely a prison," I answered. I'd seen every kind of prison imaginable, and this had all the earmarks of one. Another flash of intuition from the Goddess hit me, and my eyes flicked to one particular door. I walked over to it, Ariana following close behind. "Someone's in here that we're supposed to find."

"What?" Ariana asked in surprise. "You never said anything about rescuing someone! When were you going to tell me about this?"

I examined the keypad on the wall and the sliding shutter in the door. "I didn't know about it myself. I take orders from the Goddess, and she shows me things," I smiled ruefully, "though not always things that make my life easier. I don't know who's in here, but I have a strong feeling we need to look into it. So we will."

Ariana's eyes were wide as she stared at me. Then they narrowed. "What about Bress?"

"We'll still take care of him. Let's see what we've got to deal with." I reached up and slid the shutter open as quietly as I could to reveal the small rectangular window behind it. A quick look showed me only a bedraggled and bloody man sitting on a metal cot in the small room beyond. His dark hair was filthy and matted, and just long enough that it hung down to obscure his face. "Just one man inside. Now, how can we get in here?" I stared at the keypad. It used a number combination only, no place to swipe a card.

Ariana shifted her gaze to the keypad and thought for a moment. "Hmm," she said. Not enlightening in the least. Then she brightened. "Hang on, I have an idea." She whipped off her backpack and pulled out a small jar and a brush. Without looking at me she explained as she unscrewed the lid. "It's powdered charcoal. I use it for spells and other stuff. It's not perfect, but I think it might just work here." She gently dabbed her brush inside the jar and carefully caressed the buttons on the keypad with it. When she was done, four of the keys showed signs of use. "There you go. We know what keys, but not the order."

I looked at them carefully. There would be ten thousand combinations had we not known which four numbers were actually used. That knowledge brought the number of combinations down to twenty-four possibles. We didn't have time to try them all, and an alarm would most certainly go off if we failed the attempt. I listened silently for a moment, but the Goddess had apparently found other things to do. She wasn't helping.

Just then I heard the sound of distant footsteps from farther down the hallway and around a corner. There were a lot of them, and murmuring voices besides. I turned to look in that direction, gauging the time we'd have before they came around the corner. I heard the keypad beep four times, and when I turned back to it, its light had turned green and Ariana was reaching for the door handle. "How did you...?"

"Trade secret!" She hissed in a fierce, triumphant whisper. "Shut up and get in here!"

I couldn't help it. Behind the stone-faced expression of my glamour, I grinned.

Chapter 20

The pain was constant now, but he had resigned himself to it. Bress and his henchmen had done their job to perfection, and although his memories from before the stainless steel chamber were confused and hazy, he was certain that he had never before felt that kind of pain in his life. In the silence that had remained after Bress had left, he had found a peace of sorts. Amazingly, the constant agony had the unintended effect of clearing his mind. He still could not remember much, but he felt the press of old memories looming nearby, just at the edge of his awareness. He slowed his breathing and turned his focus inward as he tried to bring those memories into the emptiness that Bress had left in his mind. Some things slowly resolved into scenes he could recognize but not yet identify. Other, larger memories remained just out of reach, tantalizingly close. The journey back to himself would be a difficult one, but in spite of the enchanted collar and the tortures he had endured, the prisoner finally allowed a faint smile to appear on his face. He knew who he was now. Everything else would come in time.

Moments later, the prisoner frowned. Something had intruded on the fragile peace he had created within his pain. With a sigh, he opened his golden eyes, wincing as the light pierced them. Nothing had changed in the cell since Bress had left him alone, and the prisoner's brows furrowed as he tried to figure out what had disturbed him. Suddenly, there was a quiet click at the cell's only door. He recognized it as the viewing window shutter being pulled back. Someone was outside. There were two voices, one deeper than the other. They spoke briefly, and then silence fell once more. Ignoring the pain, the prisoner rose to his feet, keeping his eyes on the door. He had decided to fight them this time.

The lock clicked loudly and the door pushed inward. The prisoner crouched slightly and backed away from the opening, his hands rising into a fighting position even though he was far too weak to defend himself. The action brought a spark of memory alive, and he recalled fighting before...and winning.

Two silent figures entered, and he froze in surprise as he got his first look at them. He had expected Bress, or one of his goons, but instead he saw a young woman in black fatigues, a tactical vest, and a blonde ponytail. She carried a handgun like she knew how to use it, and she had it trained on him. She smoothly moved aside to allow another to enter the cell behind her, her finger over her lips as she bade him to stay silent. The next figure to enter was wearing a guard's uniform, but he was no guard. Even through the dampening properties of the silver collar, the prisoner could feel the tingle of magick that accompanied one of the Fae. Although his appearance was that of a nondescript young man with dark hair and stern eyes, the prisoner instantly knew better.

"Who..." his voice rasped from his bruised throat. "Who are you?"

The girl raised a finger to her lips, silently shushing him, before turning back to listen at the door. With surprising speed, she whipped a small roll of black duct tape out of her backpack and tore a piece from it. With deft fingers, she pressed the tape over the latch inside the door so that it couldn't engage, then eased it shut again. Seconds later, the sound of footsteps grew louder in the hallway only to continue past without pausing. The two stayed at the door, silent and motionless, until the hall had been empty for nearly a minute. When it was clear that they had been undiscovered, they relaxed somewhat and turned to face him. The one in the guard uniform sucked in a surprised breath.

*   *   *   *   *   *

I knew him the moment I laid eyes on him, and I couldn't believe it. In my mind, human royalty isn't worth a shit. They have power in their way through those that follow them, but I generally find them ridiculous and overly pleased with themselves. They don't know what true power is. On the other hand, Fae royalty is thick with old magick. Not bowing to them is more than foolish; it's a death sentence. Between those two extremes are those who are not Fae, but certainly not human. Supernatural creatures are far more common than most humans know, and only some of those races have an internal society that upholds their own version of a king or a queen.

And I was looking at one of the few whom I respected. He was badly injured, bloody and bruised over most of his body, and the smell of his filth was thick in the room, but I recognized him immediately. I didn't know how long he had been here, but it could have been weeks. He was thin, his wiry muscles displayed on his emaciated frame, and his eyes were wide with uncertainty and confusion. Ariana still had her gun pointed at him, and I gently put my hand on top of it and eased it down and away from him. Ariana looked surprised, but did not fight me and instead slipped the gun in its holster on her hip.

"Majesty," I said, bowing deliberately from the waist, certainly not willing to go as far as kneeling. Surprisingly, he only blinked and looked from me to Ariana and back again as if trying to make sense of what was happening. I had not seen him in many years, but there was no mistaking the golden eyes that regarded me.

Ariana's eyebrows rose surprisingly high as she looked at the bedraggled man in the corner, then at me, and then back to him once more. "*He's* a king?" Disbelief was evident in her voice. "The king of what? The homeless?"

I glared at her hard enough to make her fall silent and decided not to answer right away. For the moment, my main concern was the man in front of me. He had obviously been tortured, and kept hidden away in this cell for quite some time. If I had a human heart, it might have broken for him. As it was, I was infuriated.

He was covered in blood and grime, and his wasted body was shaking. They had left him in a thin pair of athletic shorts, and nothing else. His hair had grown long, and his beard was tangled and matted with blood, but no matter how dirty his face might have been, the eyes gave it away. Ignoring Ariana, I slowly moved closer to him, trying to be as unthreatening as possible.

"You..." his voice was raspy from disuse. "You know who I am?"

"Yes sir," I answered him as calmly as I could. I knew that time was going to run away from us quickly, but judging by the terrible state he was in, I did not wish to rush him until I had to. "I assume that Bress captured you somehow? And threw you in here?"

The man simply nodded. He took a deep, shuddering breath and sat down shakily on the nearby cot. He clasped his hands together as if realizing he was in no danger, and leaned forward, exhausted. Moments passed, and finally he spoke. "Yes," he whispered, "the fiend drugged me. I did not think that was possible, but I was apparently incorrect in that assumption. When I awoke here, I figured he wanted something, or else he would have simply killed me, and I was right." His eyes grew vague and he started to slowly shake his head side to side. His voice took on an alarmingly distant quality. "I'll never give him what he wants, never. He can't have it. He's not worthy. Never give him that. Never never never..." His voice trailed off, but he continued shaking his head.

It was Ariana who moved first. She slipped past me like a ghost, slid onto the hard bunk next to him and put her arm around his thin shoulders. He flinched from her touch for a moment, and then relaxed into her arms. She spoke to him in a soft, soothing voice, "It's gonna be all right. Whatever it is he wants, we won't let him have it. No way. We're going to get you out of here. Aren't we Kane?" She looked up and her eyes met mine rather pointedly. "Aren't we?" she repeated.

I nodded. I had already made up my mind that we had to get the prisoner to safety as quickly as possible. I had no idea what Bress wanted with him, but knowing that he had already killed a dozen women to gather energy for some enormous undertaking did not bode well. Whatever he wanted from this man would be terribly important. And no matter what it was, I would die before I let him have it.

"We're going to have to split up," I said. "I don't see a way around it." I could see Ariana begin to protest but I held up my hands in an attempt to reassure her. "Look, we were lucky to get this far. We're not going to get any farther if we take him with us, so we can't do that. We can't leave him here, though. You *have* to get him out." I paused for a moment before continuing, knowing what was coming. "I'll handle Bress."

Ariana's eyes blazed with sudden anger. "Have you lost your *mind*?" Ariana hissed. "If Bress is going down, I'm going to be there!" I could feel her fury rising. "He had all those women killed, and tried to kill me too! I owe that bastard!"

"I know, and he'll pay. I'll make sure of it." I glanced towards the prisoner and nodded in his direction. I lowered my voice to a conspiratorial whisper. "Look...he needs you. And I have a strong suspicion that taking him out of here is going to put a massive kink in whatever Bress is planning."

Ariana scowled, but didn't protest further. The man next to her trembled briefly, his eyes still focused on nothing. She glanced at him, then back at me. Her eyes narrowed and her voice echoed in my mind. *Who is this guy?*

He's the werewolf. I saw no reason to hide it from her any longer. She needed to know.

Her eyes widened in surprise. *A werewolf? Are you kidding?*

I sighed and shook my head slightly. *No. He's THE werewolf. The original. Or at least old enough that they consider him as such. He's their king, and more powerful than both of us put together.* I glanced at the exhausted, battered man sitting next to her and added, *Well...ordinarily.*

I knelt and looked into his eyes, noting that they were drowsy and unfocused. To Ariana, I said softly, "His name is Maximus Lucanis Von Gerhardt. You could say he's the exact opposite of Bress. He's probably a billionaire, has businesses all over the world, and spends a ton of his money fighting for conservation, animal welfare, reforestation, and human rights issues. Bottom line is that he's one of the good guys."

Ariana smirked. "You sound impressed."

I nodded slowly. "I am. I've seen the worst of humans over the centuries, all over the world. Their cruelty and pettiness never surprises me anymore. Men like this one, though...they're rare. He's worth saving, and especially so because Bress wants him for some reason."

Turning to the man next to her, Ariana asked quietly, "What does he want from you?"

At first, he didn't answer. Then he mumbled something that made my breath catch in my throat. Ariana asked him to repeat it, and my fears were confirmed.

"He wants..." the king's voice sounded old and tired. "He wants the Cadenstella Sword. But I won't give it to him. I won't tell him where it is, and he can't get the information out of me. He's not capable of that, no matter how strong he makes himself." A dry chuckle turned into a spasm of coughing that seemed to weaken the man further. "But he thinks he can make me talk if he hurts me enough." He fell silent and looked up at me with the golden eyes of a wolf. "He's wrong, though." His eyes flickered, and for a moment, I saw the exhaustion of the man slip aside to reveal something deeper. In that instant, I caught a flash of immense power held forcibly in check. A ferocious beast of spirit lay slumbering behind those shining eyes. I almost stepped back instinctively, but I managed to hold my ground. He sighed and continued, "I'm stronger than he thinks. I'll die before I give up the sword. And since he's not strong enough to kill me..." he spread his arms wide, displaying an array of vicious bruises, welts, and cuts covering his entire body, "this is what happens."

"How is he able to hold you? You're far more powerful than he is, aren't you?" I needed to know. If Bress could keep someone like Maximus a prisoner, he was more of a heavy hitter than I thought.

He smiled sadly. "Yes, I am. Not only could I rip him apart in my beast form, but I'm much more adept at certain magicks than he is. That's why he used this." He lifted one shaking hand to point at the silvery circlet around his neck. "It suppresses my ability to change, as well as isolating me from any magick I might use. Drugs and hunger keep me weak. Only the beast in me has kept me alive, I fear."

I reached out and carefully touched the bloodstained collar, running my fingertip over the ugly runes inscribed on its surface. My skin stung from the brief contact, and my head swam for an instant as the collar's dampening properties tried to work on me. I pulled my finger away and quickly regained my focus. "Ariana, get him out of here. Take him somewhere safe and try to get that collar off without hurting him. I'll come and find you when I'm done here."

Ariana's eyes blazed with anger, but the man next to her groaned and her rage softened. She sighed heavily and realized that I was right. She would have to get him out. Her lips compressed into a thin line, but she nodded her assent. "All right, then. I can get him out the way we came in, I think.

They'll be looking for intruders coming up, not down. Hopefully, that'll work in our favor." She stood and slipped her pack off her shoulders so that she could dig into it. In moments, she came up with a small bundle that turned out to be a close-fitting set of black athletic tights. She handed them to the king, who began to slowly put them on. As an afterthought, she reached in and pulled out an energy bar and a bottle of water, which made the king's eyes widen more than the clothing had. He gratefully accepted the food and water and immediately tore into it. To me, Ariana said, "I haven't heard of that sword. What's the deal?"

I silently debated how much to tell her, but she was already in it up to her neck, and risking herself at every turn. "The sword was made from something that fell from the stars a very long time ago. I don't know who forged it, or how, but it has a long and bloody history. It can cut through anything. Seriously, goes through armor plate as if it's nothing but butter. No one has ever been able to create a ward that could stop it either. It has other properties, too, but that's its main strength. It can kill anything."

Ariana thought about that for a moment. "Yeah, that sounds like something we don't want Bress to have." She glanced over her shoulder at the king, who was finishing up his protein bar. "OK, I'll get him out of here. I'm open to suggestions."

I thought for a moment, then said, "I can cast a glamour on you both, but it will fade pretty quickly, especially as you increase the distance between us. You're on your own after that." I handed her the keycard I had taken from the guard. "Take this, too."

Ariana nodded as she took the card. "Got it. Once I get a few floors down, I'll figure something out." She performed a quick check on both of her handguns, reseated them in their holsters, and gave me a terse nod.

"Good," I said. Against my better judgement, I was really beginning to like this human. I knew full well that she didn't want to leave, but she had accepted her new mission quickly, and seemed determined to see it through. She might just survive this whole thing, and save the king in the process. To him, I said, "Are you ready to leave, Your Majesty?"

He looked up from his hands and I saw that flash in his eyes again. Although his body was still trembling, his jaw was firmly set. He nodded. "I am, kind sir. I would lend you my strength in this, had I any to give. I am embarrassed at my frailty."

"Your Majesty, you were drugged, captured, starved, and tortured. I think we can agree that you're not exactly at your best," Ariana suggested.

He chuckled softly, "Thank you for that." He downed the last of the water, laid the food wrapper and empty bottle on the cot, then pushed himself slowly to his feet. Although hunched in pain and exhaustion, he was still taller than either of us. He wavered slightly before recovering his balance, but he took a deep breath, then nodded. "All right. I'm ready."

I moved to the door and *listened* for a moment. Nothing. I cracked the door open, dimmed myself, and poked my head into the hallway beyond. It was quiet and deserted. I turned to see Ariana standing close by, supporting King Maximus with his right arm over her shoulders. I held up a finger to stop them, and then cast as strong a glamour as I could upon them. Their bodies became as shadows, hazy and indistinct. The spell would gently guide unknowing eyes away from them even as it hid them from sight. It wouldn't last long, but if they hurried, they'd make it almost to the ground floor before it dissipated. "All right, go! Go now!" I whispered. I pulled the door open and their shadowy figures disappeared through it. I stepped out behind them and pulled the tape from the door latch, and allowed it to click shut again. I smiled, imagining how upset Bress would be when he came to check on his prisoner only to find an empty, locked cell. I smiled even more when I realized that, if I succeeded, he'd be too dead to check on him at all.

I looked down the hallway in the direction Ariana had gone, but saw nothing. She had escaped around the corner with the king, and was beyond my help now. I turned to look in the other direction. My target was waiting for me. My claws slipped out of the tips of my fingers. This time, I didn't retract them. Moving at full speed at last, I bolted silently up the hallway, determined to separate Bress's head from his body at the first available opportunity.

Chapter 21

With Ariana gone, I sprinted through the hallways at full speed, nothing more than a blur to anyone who might have been watching. Although I knew I would make much better time without her, I suddenly felt the lack of her presence. I thought of the vision the Goddess had sent me. Ariana and I had been working together for only a short time. But now she was gone, and I found myself concerned about that fact. Odd.

There was another branch up ahead that turned to the left, and I followed it, reasoning that it would bring me closer to the private staircase we had seen on the map. I came up to another door, and I leaned close to it, *listening*. When I heard nothing on the other side, I gently turned the knob and pushed it open a crack to reveal another hallway. I poked my head through and saw the room from where the lab-coated man had emerged at the far end of the hall to my left. No one was around.

I moved into the hall and headed deeper into the darkness to my right, presumably following the same path as Lab Coat. Up ahead, I could see lights illuminating an elevator. Behind those doors would be an elevator shaft. I grinned. As I approached it, I passed the door marked as a stairway, and stopped. I looked from the door to the elevator and back again. This door didn't have an electronic lock. I tried the door, and it opened easily to reveal a set of stairs leading upwards. I cast one longing glance back at the elevator, and finally conceded that

Ariana's idea was better than mine. I carefully closed the door so that it made no sound, and made my way upward.

As I headed up the stairs, I began to prepare myself for what might lay ahead. If this was Bress's inner sanctum, he would either have it heavily guarded, or not at all, thinking he was completely secure. As much as I might hope for that scenario, I knew that my luck was never that good. He would have something awful for me to get through before I could reach him. My challenge was to get as close to him as possible before the shit hit the fan, as they say.

I reached out with my senses to search for wards as I climbed the stairs, but found nothing. Bress would feel safe up here, the arrogant shit. There was a strong, oily feel of dark magick, though. The farther up I went, the worse it got, and by the time I reached the top, I felt like I needed to bathe. I'm no stranger to dark magick, but ultimately, I'm born of the Light. Bress was definitely meddling with some nasty stuff up here.

The door at the top of the stairs wasn't locked, but even as I approached, I could hear quiet voices on the other side. They were human, at least. I pressed up against the cold steel of the door and reached through it with my senses, hoping to get a better idea of what lay beyond. I *listened*. Two heartbeats became clear, both sturdy and strong, as well as the faint smell of gun oil. Judging from the amount of it I detected in the air, the men were heavily armed. As I listened, one of them spoke into his communicator, letting someone else know that all was clear. If I didn't take them out quickly, they would most certainly alert everyone else, and I did not want that.

I quietly eased open the door a crack so that I could see them, and I reached into their minds to reassure them that everything was all right. Both of them sighed heavily and I felt the tension leave their bodies. I then added the idea that they were tired and sleepy, definitely up far past their bedtime. They slumped a bit more, and their chins lowered as they slipped into a half-doze. Moving as quietly as only I could, I opened the door and stepped toward them.

The two goons were standing scant inches away, their heads nodding sleepily towards their chests. They were hardened and muscular, and definitely looked as though they could handle themselves. Both held assault rifles across their chests, ready for use, and their tactical gear fairly bristled with extra ammunition and other toys. Fortunately, they were practically asleep on their feet. I moved inside the open door and raised one hand, preparing to kill them both with one vicious swipe. Then I paused, sighed, and slammed their heads together hard enough to crack both their skulls without shattering them. The two men fell in a boneless heap on the floor, utterly still and silent.

Why did I do that? I quietly asked myself. I've been killing men like this for centuries, why would I not simply kill these and leave their bleeding bodies behind as a warning to others? Rather than spend time contemplating my sudden decision, I dragged both men away from the door where they wouldn't easily be found. Then I pulled zip ties from their utility belts and secured them to each other in the most uncomfortable fashion I could devise. I gagged them with strips torn from their shirts, then removed their communication devices, one of which I smashed. I pulled the tactical vest from the smaller guard and put it on myself so I would have a place to attach the other communicator. It wouldn't hurt to have a little extra protection against bullets either, I reasoned. I made sure I knew how the communicator worked, stuck the tiny earpiece in my ear, and muted the microphone. It was silent for the moment.

That task completed, I left the two men behind and moved farther into Bress's lair. It might have been a penthouse suite, but in truth, that's what it was: a lair. I had entered many such places, and although this one was richly appointed, it was where a foul creature had made its den. I looked forward to leaving it far behind once my job was done. *Hell,* I thought, *maybe I should set it on fire afterwards.* Then I dismissed the thought. There could be innocents in the building. Janitors aren't usually collaborators with rich, evil businessmen.

I looked around and confirmed that this was most certainly where Bress spent his time. The floor was marble and soft carpet, and the furniture looked much more appropriate for lounging than having a board meeting. Each wall had an enormous flat screen TV on it, and artwork decorated the walls at tastefully chosen intervals. I stalked forward, keeping myself dim as I went. The sound of running water caught my attention and I skirted the large interior chamber until I spied its source: a huge fountain in the next room. Beyond that lay a wide balcony, open to the stars. I recognized it from the Sprite's memories. I was definitely in the right place.

The Sprites had managed to bypass the outer Wards with ease. They had alighted on this balcony to admire the fountain before moving inside. From them, I knew that Bress had a huge office off to my left, and living quarters to my right. They had made it into his office before being discovered, and that's when Bress had attacked them. The bastard.

He had caught Larea in a sophisticated spell that froze her in midair long enough for him to blast her against the wall. I was glad that they had escaped further injury. Sprites are resilient, but that still chapped my hide. You just don't go around blasting the Sprites, even if they are being nosy.

The one thing that piqued my attention was that he had a hidden door in a bookcase on one wall. He had been entering his office from that unknown chamber when the Sprites arrived, and I had caught a glimpse of what could have been a casting room. Either I would catch him there and kill him, or if he wasn't in residence, I would make the room unusable so he could no longer perform rituals there. A petty inconvenience, but still somewhat satisfying. My guess was that he would be there, though. Good. So much the better.

Moving carefully and reaching out with my senses to find any wards before I tripped them, I padded across the marble floor and past the fountain. The wall to the office was glass, and I could see that it was empty for the moment. A massive desk dominated the space, and it was surrounded by stately bookcases filled with leatherbound books I'm sure Bress had never opened. In each corner stood a golden statue, each a stunning, three-quarter sized sculpture of a man or woman. Their lithe and muscular figures were frozen in impressive gymnastic poses, and I had to admit that the artist had been highly skilled. Aside from their silent presence, I detected no one else nearby. I tried the door, and it swung open. Scanning the office carefully, I crossed the threshold, my claws ready for action. Nothing jumped out at me and no alarms went off.

I took three steps into the middle of the room, and that's when the ward got me. It was a thing of terrible beauty, completely invisible to my senses until I touched it. That's when pain the likes of which I couldn't describe hit me like a lightning bolt that wouldn't end. I stood there, frozen in mid stride, every muscle locked in unendurable agony, and I was powerless to do anything but endure it.

Shit. Not good.

I heard and felt a thump from somewhere behind me, soon followed by others. Slow, heavy footsteps approached from either side behind me, and I saw the knickknacks on the desk shake and rattle as whatever unseen guards Bress had left headed my way. My heart sank. This was going to be a long night.

I gathered every bit of Fae strength I could muster and flung myself back and away from the ward. I managed to detach myself from it, stagger back two steps, then fall rather unceremoniously on the floor in complete agony. Wow, that hurt. I lay there, gasping in pain and trying to gather the strength to stand and fight. It was futile. I just grunted and rolled over onto my side. The ward Bress had left for me had been, as they say, a doozy.

Cold, metallic hands encircled both of my wrists and dragged me to my knees before I could find the strength to pull away. I glanced to either side and saw that two of the statues had left their pedestals and now held me in their unbreakable golden grip. *Just great,* I thought. *Golden golems.*

My claws would be even less effective on their metal bodies than they had been against the stone skin of the gargoyles. They were immune to my glamours, and completely under Bress's control. They would follow the last commands he had given them, and follow them to the absolute letter. Mindless, but stubborn, golems are.

I tried to dislodge their grip, but as strong as I usually am, the ward had temporarily knocked most of the fight out of me. Honestly, even had I been at my best, the golems' grip was unbreakable. I couldn't escape. A weak growl of frustration escaped me.

I figured Bress would appear right away to see what he had captured, but he didn't. I knelt there in his office, held fast by the short metal guards, my mind racing. I had to escape.

An idea hit me just then. Golems were immune to my attempts to influence their minds because they had none. They were animated by power Bress had invested in them. It might still be possible to fool them, though.

A shimmer passed over my body and I suddenly looked every inch a businessman. Where I had been now knelt Elias Bress himself, a recreation drawn from my own memory and augmented by every bit of my Fae magick. I imagined the voice I had heard while he blasted the Sprites and adjusted my own to match it, making it slightly higher and more nasal, but with a thick undercurrent of entitlement and contempt. It had to be perfect.

My Bress-face sneered and turned to glare at the golem on my right. "Well?" I growled in his voice, "Are you going to let me go or am I going to melt you into a puddle, you idiot?"

The golden automaton silently stared at me, no expression on its cherubic face. It was as still as any statue could be. And then its fingers opened and it released my wrist, much to my relief. I snapped a command at the other golem, and it, too, released me. "Get back to your posts, both of you! You passed my test this time, you worthless lumps!"

With heavy, thumping steps, they plodded back to their pedestals and resumed their former poses. I moved to one of them and carefully ran my fingers over its surface until I found what I knew had to be there: a tiny wad of yellow clay at the base of the statue's neck. Within that pea-sized mass would be a hair from Bress' head and a drop of his blood. When infused with his magick, it had formed the mystical connection necessary for him to transmit his will and animate the golems. I carefully scraped the clay off, rendering the statue immobile, and did the same to the other golem. The two beads of clay went into a pocket in the tactical vest I had ganked from the guard. That kind of magick wasn't my forte, but I'd seen Ariana's style, and if I didn't rip Bress' head from his shoulders tonight, we might end up needing it. Better safe than sorry, I suppose.

I moved back to the center of the room, standing just beyond where I knew the ward had hit me. I was still cloaked as Bress. I thought of the blood and hair in my pocket and wondered if that, combined with my glamour, would suffice to fool the ward. It was a longshot, but worth a try. Of course, I could also end up suffering the same agonizing effects of the ward a second time, but I could survive that, I was pretty sure.

I looked past the big desk, noting the position of the bookcase that hid his conjuring room. If he was anywhere tonight, he would most likely be in there. My claws ached a little, the thought of gutting a guy like Bress apparently pleasing to them. Hopefully, I'd have the chance to make them even happier, and soon.

The ward had been placed as a wall all the way across the office. I focused on my glamour, willing it to be as complete as I could make it in spite of the fatigue that still filled my battered body. I held my head high, as Bress would, squared my shoulders, and walked confidently toward the desk. My ridiculously large desk. I was Elias Bress, and this was my office. I belonged there.

The ward hit me with a gentle zap of static electricity, and then I was safely through it. The doorway to his casting room was only a few steps away. A wicked grin crossed my version of Bress's face. Now, I could get to work.

Chapter 22

"May I just call you Max?" Arianna whispered to the werewolf king. "It's kind of a chore to keep calling you 'Your Majesty' all the time."

He chuckled softly and wheezed, "My dear, since you're taking the trouble to help me escape, you may call me anything at all." He stumbled along beside her, his arm around her shoulders keeping him upright. He was wracked with hunger, fatigue, and pain from a thousand hurts, and although a part of him wanted nothing more than to lie down and die, the smoldering fire of his spirit pushed him onward.

Ariana nodded, "OK, good. First names all around. Just call me Ariana. I'll get you out of here and then we'll see about that thing on your neck." The king murmured something in the affirmative and continued his forward shuffle.

They reached the door that led back to the waiting area, and Ariana leaned the king against the wall. Seeing her hand as a hazy and indistinct shape was unsettling, but she was glad for Kane's glamour. She hoped it would last long enough for her to get the king to safety. Moving as quietly as she could, she turned the knob and opened the door a crack so she could peek out. The faint sewer smell they had detected before hit her, confirming their location. Her eyes drifted over the leather furniture and ornate fixtures in the room, but there was nothing that had not been there before. On the far side of the room, the frosted glass partition separated them from the burly guard Kane had left dozing. As she watched, the big man leaned back and stretched, then sat up more alertly in his chair as his senses came back online. She heard him use his communicator to check in with the other guards throughout the building, getting a bored 'all clear' from each of them. She saw him reach out and touch the pistol on his desk, then the short-barreled rifle, as if to be certain they were still within easy reach. Reassured, he leaned back in his chair, pulled out a tablet, and began tapping at it.

"Damn it," she muttered, "he's awake. And veiled or not, I doubt we can get past without him seeing. Gonna have to do this the hard way." To the king, she whispered, "Stay here." Maximus nodded and slid down the wall into a sitting position. Ariana opened the door and slipped noiselessly into the plush lounge. She crept towards the frosted glass partition, staying low to avoid the guard's line of sight. Her mind raced as she tried to figure out a way to deal with him. Gunshots would alert the entire floor. She would have to find another way. When she reached the glass wall, she pulled out the keycard they had taken earlier. Crouching on her knees, she reached up and swiped the card across the face of the reader and froze in place.

The reader beeped and the indicator glowed green on both sides, instantly alerting the guard beyond. He snatched up the handgun from his desk and whirled at the sound, his steely eyes scanning for an intruder. His eyes lingered on Ariana's hazy outline for a moment or two, but there apparently wasn't enough there to keep his attention. He looked at the keypad only to see that it had already gone red again. He tried the door with his left hand and found it locked as it should have been. He looked around a moment longer, then holstered the gun and shook his head.

"Damned glitchy tech," Ariana heard him mutter. She waited until he began to turn away, then she swiped the card again. It beeped cheerily and the guard's head snapped back around. He pulled his gun, cursed, and pushed open the door. Keeping his gun at the ready, he moved deliberately into the waiting area, his eyes darting left and right as he scanned the room for intruders. Focused as he was on the middle of the room, his eyes skipped right over Ariana's indistinct form. For a moment. Then he stopped as if frozen. His eyes slowly cut back to where she knelt and he stared, trying to figure out what he was looking at. His expression hardened as he finally saw the girl beneath the shadowy glamour, and his gun shifted towards her.

Ariana burst into action, exploding out of her crouch. In one smooth motion, she reached out with her left hand and grabbed the gun as she turned her body sideways to avoid the shot if it came. Her right fist slammed into the guard's face like a machine piston before joining her other hand on the gun. Her body slammed into his, pinning his arm between them and making him stagger back a step. With a sharp yank, she wrenched the gun out of his hand and reversed the grip as she stepped away. In an instant, she had assumed a shooter's stance with the gun leveled at a spot right between the guard's eyes. He wavered, but stayed on his feet, recovering quickly from the hard punches to the face.

"Hands up. Say a word and you die right now," Ariana hissed in a tight whisper.

The guard's mouth was open, but after a moment's thought, he closed it. His hands rose slowly and carefully. Blood trickled from his right nostril and his nose was already swelling. He stood that way for a beat, then raised one eyebrow, as if asking, "What next?"

"Down on the floor, hands behind your back. Nothing funny. You know the drill, don't you big guy?"

He sighed and nodded. Keeping his hands up, he slowly went down on one knee, and then surprised her by springing forward faster than she had thought possible. His hands grabbed hers, struggling for the gun. They grappled for it and she fell on her back as his weight hit her. She knew she only had seconds before noise of the scuffle would draw attention, and that was if he didn't manage to call for help first.

Flinging the gun away to keep it out of his reach as well as free up her hands, Ariana surprised the thug by pulling him closer. Pulling her knees up to her chest, she insinuated her legs between their bodies, pushing and pulling with her feet until she was able to fling her right leg around his neck. She pulled his right arm sharply between her thighs, quickly folded her other leg over her right foot, and squeezed her knees together as tightly as she could.

The guard's eyes widened as he realized he was in a triangle choke, and it was a good one. He frantically pulled at her legs with his hands as the pressure inside his head quickly increased. He had a vague thought of picking her up and slamming her to the ground, but it was already far too late. His eyelids fluttered, closed, and then a loud, gurgling snore escaped his throat as he passed into unconsciousness. Ariana held the choke a bit longer just to be safe, then she unwound her legs and released him, kicking him over so he flopped bonelessly onto his back.

"Geez, you run about, what, two-sixty? Big fellow. It's a shame you're a bad guy. You're kinda cute, in a big, lunkheaded kind of way." Ariana pulled some zip ties from one of her many pockets. She looked over his swollen, bloodied face, then amended, "Well, you were, anyway." Moving efficiently, she hogtied and gagged him before pulling his body off to one side and stowing it behind one of the couches. She stripped his body of communications gear and weapons, finding another tiny pistol in an ankle holster as well as a pair of knives secreted about his body. Just to be safe, she quickly cast a gentle sleep spell to keep him quiet. When he was situated, she stood, then as an afterthought, bent down and patted his muscular backside. "Nice butt, though," she muttered. Then she briskly walked over to the door where she had left the king.

She pushed open the door to find him dozing just where she had left him. "OK, Max, let's roll."

He blinked bleary eyes, then slowly got to his feet, accepting her assistance as he did so. "Trouble?" he asked.

"Nah," Ariana replied. "Nothing I couldn't handle. C'mon, let's get out of here before someone comes and finds Tiny over there."

Maximus looked over at the brute Ariana had just bundled up, and shook his head. "You are a formidable young lady, Miss Ariana. I am fortunate to have met you."

"Thanks," Ariana said with a smile. "Let's get moving while we have the chance."

They moved up to the glass wall, where she swiped her card again, turning the indicator light on the lock green once more. As they passed by the desk, Ariana's eyes dropped to the guard's short-barreled AR-15, still leaning where the guard had left it. "Hold on," she said, briefly leaving Max to stand on his own while she snagged the gun and stuffed it into her backpack. She opened the drawers in the desk and came up with two straight magazines and one heavy drum, all full of ammunition. Those somehow went into the pack as well. "Might come in handy," she said as she slid her arms back into the straps of her pack.

The king's golden eyes regarded her with both amusement and approval. "Indeed, my lady. They just might. My powers are currently denied me, but I can still shoot one of those."

"Good to know," she replied, replacing his arm over her shoulders. She started towards the stairwell door, then realized that there would be a pair of guards on the other side. She doubted they could sneak past them a second time, especially without Kane's ability to cloud their minds. She stopped and eyed the elevator as she worked through her options.

The veil Kane had placed on them was still working, rendering their bodies shadowy and indistinct, but even so, they wouldn't be able to just walk through a brightly lit lobby full of guards without being noticed. Once someone paid close enough attention, they'd be able to see them just as the last guard had. They would need a diversion, at the very least. If they used the elevator, it would show up on someone's screen. Then her eyes widened.

"Wait! Hold on one sec," she whispered as she left Max to stand on his own. Ariana darted back to the guard's desk and checked his monitors. Surely enough, one of them was split into several views, each showing the inside of an elevator. They would certainly have been seen, but only if the guard wasn't currently tied up on the floor in the room beyond. "Hot damn, we've got this! This guy was watching the elevators. With him out of the way, we can use them without anyone else seeing us. They're clear now; we can take one down."

Just then, something on another screen caught her eye. A guard was moving down a hallway leading...she squinted and leaned forward to confirm what she was seeing...yes, it was an entire horde of goblins. "Ew," she muttered. She had not come up against goblins often, but in her experience, they were strong and fierce beasts. "And they stink," she added, speaking mostly to herself. She checked the tag on the video window and saw that the feed was from the first floor. The guard had opened the door at the end of the hallway and was standing aside while the goblins jostled and pushed their way through the portal. It seemed to take forever for them all to get through, but finally, the guard followed the last goblin inside and let the door slowly fall closed behind them. She rolled her eyes in disgust. "Ugh. Looks like we won't be going out that way." Shaking her head, she left the monitors and moved back to the king. "The elevators are clear, but we can only go as far as the second floor."

Maximus grimaced, but replied simply, "That's progress, at the very least. I'm ready when you are." He put his arm back around Ariana's shoulders and let her support him to the elevators. She reached out and punched the down button, and the doors opened right away.

"Just stay close," she said as they moved inside. The doors slid closed and she pushed a button. "Maybe we can find a way out on two. At that height, we might be able to just break out a window and make a run for it. They're looking for someone approaching, not someone trying to get out." The elevator started to move, and she began running through scenarios in her mind. None of them felt particularly good.

Suddenly, the elevator emitted a cheery 'ping!' Startled, Ariana's eyes flashed to the digital readout over the door. It said '5.' She grabbed the king, shoved him into the corner next to the door but away from the control panel, and covered his body with her own. As the door slid open, she looked down to see that their bodies were still somewhat shadowy and transparent, but growing more visible all the time.

Five uniformed guards walked in, chatting excitedly with each other, but paying no attention to the dimly seen fugitives in the corner. They were embroiled in a discussion about goblins, and everyone had a lot to say. Ariana gave one fellow a carefully timed push, deftly reaching out with one foot and tipping one of his feet into the other. The guard stumbled hard into his comrades, eliciting grunts of surprise and a loud, "Hey, what the hell, man!"

Taking advantage of their momentary distraction, Ariana latched onto King Maximus and pulled him close. Staying close to the doors, she rolled them both around the corner and out of the elevator, where the guards were now arguing heatedly and harassing the one she had tripped.

"Jesus, Denny, you're the clumsiest dude I ever saw," one said.

"Stick it, Robert, somebody tripped me!"

A chorus of denials and laughter erupted from the others, suddenly silenced by the closing of the elevator doors. Ariana looked around to take stock of their situation.

They had exited into a small waiting area with a few chairs, a couch, and some small potted trees and plants. Ariana pulled the king down with her behind the nearest potted shrub while she spied out their surroundings, staying ready just in case the guards returned.

When she was sure the elevator doors wouldn't open again, she sighed and sat on the floor with the king seated next to her. "Well," she said, keeping her voice quiet, "fifth floor is better than fifteenth, I guess."

"Still higher than I can jump right now," Maximus offered apologetically. "I'm sorry for my weakness."

"Back up," Ariana said, "what do you mean, 'right now?' You mean you could ordinarily survive a jump from five floors up?"

The king chuckled sadly. "Indeed. Sometimes farther, if I'm rested and highly motivated. Motivated I might be, but rested...not at all. I am sorry."

Ariana shook her head, impressed. "Hey, no sorries necessary, Max. Not your fault. Let's see if we can find another way down."

They stood up, and then they heard a faint whirring sound from somewhere nearby. Ariana barely had time to put her hand on the butt of her gun before the source of the noise rolled around the corner.

"Ah, hell," was all Ariana had time to say before things went from bad to really bad.

Chapter 23

This place disgusted me. Everything about it spoke of decadence and human avarice. Gold curtains, giant mahogany desk, expensive leather everywhere. It was excessive, but then again, I expected no less of a business magnate like Elias Bress. I'd hold anyone like him in contempt, but otherwise, they would generally be beneath my notice. Bress was different, though. He was meddling in affairs better left alone. Anyone dealing with the darker powers ran the risk of not only losing their own lives and souls, but the trouble they could bring about wasn't necessarily limited to just the idiot who started the problem. I've had to put down quite a few overambitious sorcerers in my day, lest they unleash some extremely unsavory creatures into our dimension. I had a strong desire to add Bress to that list, thus preventing that kind of nonsense.

The place practically stank of dark magick. Humans would never have known, other than feeling a certain heaviness, a sense of oppression and hopelessness, if they spent too much time in Bress's office. I had no doubt that he had used that to his advantage.

I walked over to the bookcase I had seen in Tatyana's memory. The oily feel of his magick was thicker there, and I knew that his conjuring room lay just beyond. I just had to figure out how to get inside. Staying as quiet as I could, I rummaged through the bookcase, moving things around and sliding my hands along the shelves as I looked for the hidden catch that opened the door. Rather than the old 'pull-the-book' switch, Bress had opted for a simple pushbutton under one of the shelves. I pressed it, and the bookcase slid noiselessly open. Everything was still and quiet, so I slipped inside.

The room beyond was dark, but the smells of blood, incense, and brimstone overpowered the lemony pine smell of the office behind me. I'm no stranger to the dark. The details of the room began to reveal themselves almost immediately as my eyes adjusted. Although still weak from the beating I had taken from the ward, I was eager to get this whole thing over with. I took a few cautious steps forward.

That was a mistake.

My eyes are Fae. I can see in almost no light. Unfortunately, shifting from complete darkness to intensely bright, blinding light is still problematic, even for me. As I heard the door behind me loudly click shut, everything in the room went completely white as high powered lights came on, freezing me for one crucial moment. That's all it took. Something whipped around my arms and legs, pinning them together. The pain cranked up immediately, and I heard myself cry out as the immovable bands began to burn my skin. I tried to stay on my feet, but with everything bound so tightly, I finally fell to one side. I landed hard on my right shoulder, then I rolled to my back, clenching my teeth to keep from screaming. It almost worked.

"Well, well, I see you're a fellow practitioner." The oily voice could only have belonged to Bress. "Otherwise, you'd never had made it past my ward. I have to say that your veil is extraordinary. You almost look like me, even now." Bress walked over to the wall and turned a dimmer switch to lower the lights to a more normal level.

I blinked the tears out of my eyes, and they finally adjusted completely. I saw mostly what I expected from a rich man's conjuring room, though it was far neater than many I had seen. Where others had all of their spellcrafting supplies in mismatched bottles and jars, organized in haphazard fashion, Bress had spared no expense in setting up his conjuring space. It looked more like a lab than a spell casting room. The floors were black marble with gold inlays, and a huge black desk sat off to one side with a small wooden chest on its polished surface. One wall was lined with cabinets and shelves, all meticulously labeled in gold lettering, and I could see an array of bottles with all sorts of powders, leaves, and other substances.

The thing that concerned me more was the altar on the far side of the room. It was black granite, and I could see multiple arm and leg restraints bolted to the stone. An aura of black magick surrounded the thing, a dense fog of pain and hatred. I had seen them here and there over the centuries, and those who used them had always come to an awful end. That said, those people had caused a lot of trouble and killed many innocents before their end finally showed up. The sight of an altar like that did not bode well.

I kept my mouth shut. I needed a moment to think, to find a way out of this. As far as I knew,

Bress had no idea that I was of the Fae. I had been using veils and glamours for hundreds of years. No matter how much he hurt me, he wouldn't see my true self unless I willed it, even if I were dead. No, he thought I was another sorcerer, likely a friend of Ariana's. I needed to keep it that way as long as possible. I didn't know what ritual he was trying to complete, but Fae blood was mighty potent in such things. He needed Ariana, but it was possible that my blood might be a viable substitute.

Two pairs of strong hands yanked me off the ground and slammed me down in a chair. Where the guards outside had been ordinary humans, these two seemed to have been created from some movie-thug mold: tall, thickly-muscled, bearded, shaved bald and sharing the same dead stare. They could have been robots for all their emotional expression. From what I could sense, they were still human, but with something extra. Bress had done something to them, though I wasn't sure what. In any event, I knew there would be no subduing either of them peacefully. I'd have to kill them, and thoroughly. Just as soon as I could get loose. I strained weakly against my bonds and tried to assess my situation.

The bands that pinned my arms and legs together turned out to be two lengths of steel cable, enchanted and animated to bind anyone deemed an intruder. It was a simple idea, but a tricky spell to control, and the pain caused by contact with the cable was an extra touch that Bress had apparently added. The Fae didn't much care for iron, but I was less vulnerable to it than most for some reason.

Some of my kin would burst into flames if iron even touched them, but I've been given a certain amount of immunity. Perks of the job, I suppose. Not that it was helping me out of my current plight, but it could have been a lot worse. The pain I was feeling was an intentional gift from Bress that he had added into the enchantment, but no more than that. I gritted my teeth together and kept quiet.

"Not talking?" Bress's smug voice drifted across the room again and I finally turned my head in his direction.

He was pouring himself a drink at a tiny bar in the corner of the room; bourbon, by the smell of it. He replaced the stopper in the cut glass decanter and carefully set the bottle back in place before picking up his glass and swirling the amber liquid around. He was dressed much as I had expected. His black suit and shirt fit his athletic body perfectly, set off by golden cufflinks that sparkled as he moved. That suit probably cost him thousands. I looked forward to getting my claws into it. The thought of ripping it, and him, to pieces suddenly made me awfully happy. I must have smiled at the thought.

He looked at me, then chuckled. "Well, I'm glad you seem to be amused. You know, I have to admit I'm impressed. By now, anyone else would be unconscious or else screaming in agony from my little surprise. Why aren't you?" He took a sip of his drink and leveled his cold gaze at me. A small smile stayed on his lips, but avoided his eyes completely. "Why aren't you?" he repeated, more softly.

I could see the wheels turning in his mind. If he figured out what I was, that might not end well for me. I had to throw him off, or at least stall him until I could think of a way out of this. Using his own voice, I finally replied, "Just lucky, I guess."

His eyes widened. "Is that what I sound like?" Bress laughed. "Marvelous! I like it. I sound quite manly, don't you think?" He sipped his drink. "Well, whoever you are, you've caused me some trouble. That was you that killed my man Luther, wasn't it? I thought it was the girl, but that had to have been you. And you brought the girl here to do what, try to stop me?" He laughed again, genuinely amused. "You've got some guts, I'll give you that. Both of you. Too bad it won't do either of you any good. I knew you were here the moment you crossed the street. I've just been waiting to see how far you would get."

I laughed, and that seemed to surprise him. "You think I didn't know that you had eyes on us? Admit it, you had no idea where we were once we got inside, did you?" His smile faltered just a bit, enough to tell me that I'd been right. I laughed again in spite of the pain still coursing through me from the cables. "You retreated here because you knew we'd end up here eventually, and you couldn't risk being caught by us anywhere you might be vulnerable."

He stared at me for just a moment, then the smile reappeared in full force as he shook his head. He took another sip from his drink and pointed one finger at me. "Touché," he said quietly. "You're right.

I lost you there for a while, but that doesn't matter. I've got you now. And when she comes for you, I'll have her too. Here, watch this."

Bress walked over to a panel on the wall next to the hidden door and touched it. It came alive with icons, and he tapped one. In a clear, authoritative voice, he spoke, "Attention. One of the intruders has been apprehended in the penthouse. Please be advised there is still one intruder somewhere in the building. That is all." He tapped the icon to close it, and smiled at me. "That announcement went over the speakers throughout the entire building. Now your friend knows where you are and that I've got you. With any luck, she'll come right up to fetch you."

I kept my face (his face, actually) neutral. With any luck, she was already outside, on her way to get Maximus to safety. Just then, another voice crackled in the earpiece I had stolen from the guard even as it came over the speaker in the wall for Bress to hear. "Be advised, we have a disturbance on five. I say again, a disturbance on five. Possible intruder, please investigate and apprehend. Gob One and his crew are en route." Then the earpiece was ripped out of my ear by thug number two, who had apparently noticed I was wearing it. That hurt a bit. I glanced over at him, imagining how I would kill him. That made me feel better, but the fact remained that Ariana was still in the building and she had heard the announcement.

"Well, that should speed things up," Bress purred, his voice smooth as oil. "Once I get her up here, then I can finish this, once and for all."

I cut my eyes towards him. My claws were just itching to slide through his flesh. I'd have happily ripped out his throat with my teeth if he'd been close enough. But the cables held me fast, and the constant pain was sapping my energy and making my head swim. Before too long, slipping into unconsciousness would be a relief, but one I could simply not afford. I had to get out of this.

In spite of the agony it caused, I sent my awareness into the cables that held me, into the magick that powered them. Although the pain made it difficult to focus, I knew that it might be possible for me to unravel the spell if I could find its fundamental structure and pick at it with my own magick. It was going to take a lot of effort, and I had no doubt that Bress was going to distract me one way or another. I needed to work quickly, but it was painstakingly slow. Ripples of shock and pain coursed through me at every turn, but I ignored them and set a part of my will to the task. Keeping my voice level, I addressed Bress. "Why her?"

He had been sipping from his drink again, but put it down and turned to face me. "Why her?" he repeated. "You know she's a witch, and a strong one, at that. Even stronger than her mother was." Oddly, his eyes got a faraway look and he paused as if remembering. Then his green gaze snapped back to me and he continued, "All of the women I ordered killed were witches, though most of them didn't know it. Their power was necessary for what I have planned."

I winced as pain shot through me again. "And what is that? What could you possibly want that you don't already have?"

He laughed. "Oh, so this is the part where I reveal my evil plan? You've been watching too many James Bond movies, I think. Telling you what I've got in mind doesn't help me in the least."

He had me there. But this wasn't my first rodeo, as they say. "I'm betting she's a sacrifice to one of the Dark Ones. What do you get in return? Power? Wealth? Guys like you always want more of that."

He shook his head. "I've got plenty of both, that's true. No, that's another goal for the long run, but what I want right now is much more important." He looked me over for a moment, then smiled broadly. "Oh, why not? I'll play the part. You want to know what the ritual will bring me? Life. That's what I want." He spread his arms and turned in a slow circle, obviously proud of himself. "My organization is enormous, worldwide. There's no corner of the globe I can't reach. I have wealth enough to buy a country if that served my purposes. But life...that's what I need more of, my friend. I want to live long enough to enjoy what I've built. I want to see my enemies die around me as I flourish and keep growing."

I tried to laugh, but the pain kept me from it. "You're asking the Dark Ones for immortality? They'll never grant you that. It doesn't serve them."

"True, but I've not asked for that, exactly. I simply asked for the ability to heal myself. To regenerate my body when it breaks down. Technically, I wouldn't be immortal, but the effect would be virtually the same thing."

I thought about it. The sacrifice of thirteen witches, whether or not they knew they had power, would count highly in his favor with many of the Dark Ones. Although I didn't know exactly which entity he had treated with, some of them could certainly grant him the ability to heal his body indefinitely, thus giving him a form of immortality. He could be around to cause trouble for centuries.

The memory of the voice I had heard coming from the mouth of Ariana's assailant suddenly arose, and I realized that it hadn't been Bress at all. It had been the power *behind* Bress. Suddenly, I realized that although Bress was trying to gain something for himself, the Demon behind him probably had something much more self-serving in mind. And no matter how bad Bress might be, letting a Demon of that magnitude loose around here would be a thousand times worse. That would suck. I had to stop Bress.

Bress must have seen the realization in my copies of his eyes because he laughed softly. "Yes, you see it now, don't you? You begin to grasp the possibilities." He began to stroll leisurely around the golden circles embedded in the floor, carefully skirting them as he walked. "Living forever would give me power beyond anything I could ever hope to accomplish in just one lifetime. Add to that the other things I've got going on, and I'll be invincible. Untouchable. The very idea is just breathtaking." He sighed with excitement, then turned back to me, his green eyes twinkling. "And I must say, there *is* a certain level of satisfaction I'm getting out of telling you my plans! I'm glad I told you." His face hardened then. "Now that we've settled all that...who sent you?"

Uh oh. I knew this moment would come. Time for the beatdown. Usually, I was the one doing the beating, though. "Your mother," I responded. "See, I'm your new stepdad. You should let me go, she's going to be pretty upset when she doesn't get her spanking tonight."

Bress froze. And then he laughed. Damn. I had hoped to piss him off. "You amuse me, stranger. All right, we'll play it that way if you like. Knut, Lars," he addressed the two muscle-heads on either side of me, "hurt him but don't kill him. I want him able to talk. He might yet be of some use to us."

Unfortunately, it's pretty hard to make me pass out. I remember everything they did. It all hurt.

Chapter 24

"Get down!" Ariana hissed in a tight whisper as she shoved Max to his knees. In his weakened state, he could not have resisted her even had he tried to do so, and quickly let gravity have its way with him. She joined him behind the potted plant again and pulled one of her Glocks, then stuffed it back in its holster with a curse. Any shots would surely alert security, and she didn't have time to dig out a silencer. She had to find another way to deal with the thing that had just rounded the corner.

It looked like a Segway, only much smaller, standing only about as high as Ariana's knees. It rode on two wheels, joined by a flat axle, and was bisected by a control stalk that supported a blocky head of sorts. It scanned its surroundings through a glass face that swiveled slowly in all directions, following its programmed pattern with unerring precision. Ariana noticed another block set just beneath the head that held several holes of different sizes. A chill ran down her spine as she recognized them for what they were: gun barrels. A second glance revealed a solid ammo belt attached to one side of the lower part of the head. A box of high-velocity rounds rested at the bottom of the belt, ready to feed the cartridges up the line.

The Sec-Bot rolled into the center of the waiting area and stopped. It turned away from them and Ariana saw its head begin to systematically scan the room, up and down, left to right. They had only a handful of seconds before its glassy face turned in their direction. She glanced down at her arm and cursed inwardly as she saw that the veil Kane had cast upon them had almost completely faded; her body was still a bit fuzzy, but plainly visible, as was the king's. She looked up again to see the Bot turned almost all the way towards them. She doubted the potted plant would shield them from its mechanically-enhanced vision. *Dammit!* she thought.

Desperate, she decided to try to distract it. One of her hands darted into the potted plant in front of her and she scooped up a handful of the decorative rocks that filled it. Keeping one eye on the bot, she flung the black stones into the hallway from which it had come. With sharp rapping sounds, they ricocheted from the wall and bounced down the hall and out of sight, rattling loudly on the floor beyond. Even before the stones impacted, Ariana ducked back behind the plant and put a hand on Max's arm. He glanced up at her and nodded. He was ready.

The Sec-Bot whirled the instant the first stone hit the far wall. There was a loud *click-clack* as the Bot's weapon charged a round into the chamber, and a bright red dot suddenly appeared on the wall opposite its glass face as the targeting laser snapped on. Its rubber wheels spun it around in place, orienting it towards the sound, then it rolled forward with alarming speed. It stopped just before the corner, and its head leaned forward and turned, spying out the space before it straightened up and rolled down the deserted hallway.

The instant the Bot disappeared, Ariana sprang into action, pulling Maximus along. They were only a few yards down the opposite hallway when Ariana heard the whirring of the Bot behind her and saw the glowing spot of the targeting laser on the wall to her right.

"Dammit," she muttered. She grabbed Max's arm and juked to her left, moving him with her, just as gunfire erupted behind her. A line of shots stitched along the wall to her right, showering her with bits of dust and sheetrock as the Sec-Bot tried to mow them down. The hairs on the back of her neck stood as she imagined the red dot of the targeting laser settling on her. She spotted a doorway up ahead to the left, and shoved the king towards it. "Get inside!" He stumbled away from her, and suddenly, her hands were free.

Ariana pulled both her guns, whirled, and dropped to her knees. Bullets tore through the air where her head had been, hissing above her like angry bees.

"My turn, R2!"

Both of her pistols bucked in her hands as she returned fire. The 9mm bullets shattered the Sec-Bot's glass face, sending it into a jerky spin. She lowered her aim and hammered a few rounds into the firing assembly for good measure, throwing it badly out of alignment. The machine shuddered and shook with each impact as it tried to right itself, but it had not been made to take return fire. It spat out a few more rounds that hit nothing but sheetrock, then its brain stalk tipped over backwards and fell to the floor. Its wheels whirred as it turned itself in a tight circle, and sparks flew from its shattered circuits. It emitted a muffled *POOF*, along with a tiny cloud of smoke, then went still.

Ariana kept her guns trained on the machine, but it stayed dead. When she was certain it wouldn't rise again, she turned to check on Max, but he wasn't there. The door she had shoved him towards was closed and quiet. "Max?" she whispered loudly enough for him to hear behind the door. "You OK in there?" In practiced, efficient motions, she switched out both magazines for fresh ones before seating her guns back in the holsters that clung to her thighs.

The door opened a crack, revealing one of Max's golden eyes. Its gaze paused on her for only a moment, then the door swung open all the way.

"Thank you," he said softly. He leaned heavily on the doorframe, obviously exhausted. "I apologize again for being such a liability. If I could get this thing off, I'd be much more help." He tugged gently at the silvery collar around his neck.

"Hey, don't worry about it," Ariana replied as she scanned the hallway to her right. "First chance I get, I'll try to get that thing off of you. It can't be comfortable..." she broke off when a smug voice suddenly blared over hidden speakers in the ceiling.

"Attention. One of the intruders has been apprehended in the penthouse. Please be advised there is still one intruder somewhere in the building. That is all."

"That would be Bress," Maximus offered. "At this point, I'd know that arrogant voice anywhere."

Ariana swore in the most unladylike fashion she could muster and shook her head in ire. "Well, that didn't take long. I thought Kane would be a little better at this than to get captured so quickly."

Maximus turned his unnerving gaze fully upon her. "You really don't know what he is, do you?"

She stopped and stared. "Sure. He's..." she frowned, "he's one of the Faerie." When she wasn't able to say more, she realized that she didn't know as much as she thought she did. "Right?"

Maximus spoke softly, "Yes, but he's a particular kind of Faerie. He's a Grim. He's quite deadly, as I'm sure you've seen."

Ariana nodded. "Yeah, he's quick. He took out some demons and some kind of zombie troll earlier. With a little help, of course." A proud smile appeared, brightening her face, and she winked.

The king laughed, "And I'm sure he was grateful. But I assure you, he's more capable than you think. I've met him before, long ago, and you'd be surprised at what he can do. But Bress," Maximus sighed and touched his collar gently, "he has some surprising resources."

Ariana looked at the collar again. The symbols inscribed on its surface made her head ache to look at them, but they seemed more familiar now that she'd had time to think on them. They almost made sense now. Suddenly, her earpiece came alive.

"Be advised, we have a disturbance on five. I say again, a disturbance on five. Possible intruder, please investigate and apprehend. Gob One and his crew are en route."

"Gob One, sir?" a different, younger voice replied over the airwaves.

"That's Collin and his goblins, newb," the first voice clapped back, annoyed. "Just stay out of their way."

"Sir, yes sir! Standing by on seven!" The intercom went silent.

Ariana rolled her eyes. "Ugh! Just can't catch a break. Come on, we've got to find a way out of here before the..." She considered what she was about to say, finding it both amusing and ironic. "Before the goblins get here."

Max made a sound that resembled a low growl. "Foul creatures, those. Ordinarily, they would only trouble me a little, but right now, I doubt I could handle many of them."

Ariana thought for a moment, then said, "Wait here." She sprinted back down the hallway to the small waiting area they had just left. She suddenly felt grateful for all the CrossFit classes she had been taking as she hauled all of the furniture up against the elevator doors, stacking the two couches on top of each other. It wouldn't slow anything determined down for long, but it would still count for something. As an afterthought, she kicked the metal corpse of the Sec-Bot up against the pile as well before heading back down the hall. She checked the stairwell door as she passed and saw that it operated on a keycard. She used her card to open it, and leaned into the stairwell. She could already hear the thumping of hundreds of feet from somewhere down below. Bestial growls and shrieks drifted up to her,

making her blood run cold. She only knew goblins
from her mother's books and a brief encounter years
ago. Even so, she had no desire to meet them in the
flesh in such numbers. She drew her knife, used the
pommel to smash the card mechanism on that side,
then ducked back out of the stairwell and let the
door swing shut. Satisfied with the loud click she
heard when it closed, she sprinted back to where
Max was waiting.

"OK, Max. Let's boogie."

Chapter 25

Pain and I are old friends. I've given out barrels of it, but let me tell you, I've taken my share over the centuries. I think I took a large percentage of it right there in Bress's conjuring room that night. I did manage to bite off three of Knut's fingers when he got careless, but other than that, they covered an awful lot of ground.

The good news is that my bones are sturdy. And they heal ridiculously quickly. But oh, Goddess, they hurt when they're breaking and they hurt while they're healing, and Knut and Lars gave me a lot of opportunities to feel it both ways.

"I must say, you're impressively durable," Bress had stayed out of the way so that his suit remained pristine. Knut and Lars were covered in my blood. "Anyone else would have died by now."

"Yes, well, I work out a little," I blubbered, "yoga and such." My painfully split lips were knitting themselves slowly back together, and itched like mad. Bress couldn't see my true features, so I made sure the image of him that I wore was suitably bloody and bruised.

"Lars, go ahead and get him up here." Bress gestured to the black altar, as I knew he eventually would. "Whatever he is, I'm sure that Shar-Nakhan will be happy with an additional offering."

Lars took a step forward, but my voice stopped him. "Hang on a minute, Bress. Maybe we can make a deal." Lars turned his head to look at his boss and raised an eyebrow, awaiting further instructions.

Bress laughed. "A deal? What could you possibly have that I want?" To Lars, he said, "Get him up there and strap him down."

As Lars' big hands grabbed me by the arms, I raised my voice, trying to add a note of desperation to the words. "I...I have the sword! I know where it is!"

Bress stood up, concern evident on his face at last. "Wait!" Lars froze in place, holding me up with my toes dangling inches from the marble floor. His blood-spattered face looked from me to Bress and back again. Bress continued, "Put him back down!"

Lars did as he was commanded and set me back in the chair. At a wave from Bress, the enormous man excused himself and slipped out the hidden door, following where the maimed Knut had gone before. Moving in no hurry, and doing his best to hide his sudden, intense interest, Bress strolled over to where I sat, picking up a stool on the way. I watched him closely, knowing that I had his full attention now. If I could just get him to come nearer, there was a slim chance I could do something. He walked towards me, but stopped himself, wisely keeping out of arm's reach even though I was still bound. Damn him for being smart. He put the stool down a couple of yards away from me and sat on it, his green eyes narrowed in calculation.

"All right, then. Talk. What sword?"

I stayed silent, giving myself every possible second to let my body heal. I endured the pain as my forearm bone finally knit itself back together and tried not to smile as I felt it become solid again. At last, I spoke. "Seriously? You know exactly what sword, you ass."

Bress blinked and stared at me. "Well, that's an interesting bluff. How could you even know I was..." his voice trailed off and then he abruptly stood and walked back over to the panel in the wall. He tapped it and spoke. "Lars. Take Knut and go check on...the prisoner."

I laughed. "Von Gerhardt is gone. I helped him escape, and in return, he told me where the sword is hidden. Let me go, and I'll tell you where it is."

Bress turned back to me, fury written plainly on his face. "Or I could just start cutting fingers off until you tell me."

"Well, that's a less attractive option, but I admit, it might work."

Bress bolted over to the huge desk, where a small chest lay waiting. He waved a hand over it and spoke a few words. I felt the pressure of the evil magick he invoked as the runes on the box flared a bright, ugly scarlet, then faded again. He hastily opened the lid and withdrew a dagger from within. I recognized it immediately. It was from the same set as the other knife I had found on the assassin, but a bit larger and more ornate. The one I had found was one of the five lesser blades from the set of six, but in his hand, he held the most powerful blade of them all. And he was probably planning to use it on me in the next minute or so.

I have to say that my job is a lot of things, but boring is not one of them.

Bress marched back over to me and brandished the knife, holding the tip a few inches from my nose. I could feel the blade's thick aura of dark magick pressing against my awareness. It had slit thousands of throats and stabbed countless hearts, sending horrified souls screaming into awful, distant realms. I had to get that thing away from him.

"All right then," Bress sneered, finally furious. "Where is it?" Baring his teeth, he flicked the blade once, opening a stinging gash in my cheek. Pain shot through my body as every fiber of my being shuddered in revulsion at the touch of the foul metal. "Tell me now or the next one is in your eye."

I looked up at him for a long moment, watching until I saw his right eye begin to twitch in anger. Perfect.

"All right, all right. I'll talk." I paused as long as I felt I safely could before continuing. I needed every second I could get. "It's not going to be...easy to reach. You'll need help."

That caught him off guard. His eyes widened and his head tilted slightly before one side of his mouth curled into a sneer. "I'm pretty sure I can handle it, you idiot. Now where is it?" He jabbed me again, barely missing my eye this time.

"Fine!" I let desperation fill my words as I flinched away from the evil blade. "All right, you'll need a few things."

"Like what?" He loomed over me, his fury rising. His face was twisted in a hideous scowl, teeth clenched. A bead of sweat rolled down one side of his face, and a vein bulged in his neck. Yes, indeed, he was pretty upset.

"The first thing you'll need," I stuttered, then mumbled the next part.

"What was that?" Bress leaned forward.

"A colonoscope."

The beat of silence as he realized where I'd just told him to look for the sword was priceless. He froze for only an instant, then I heard the angry intake of breath that I knew was coming.

And that was my moment. I flexed my arms and broke the last bit of enchantment that held the cables around my biceps. My left hand grabbed his right, clenching his fingers around the handle of the knife and sharply twisting his wrist. I popped the cables around my legs open as I lunged forward. I swiped at his neck with my right hand, claws out and ready to relieve the pressure in that vein.

Bress yelled in pain as something gave in his wrist, but he somehow flung an arm up in time to block my attack. Worse for me, my claws slammed into a ward that I hadn't even known he had. There was a bright flash as his magick shield hardened and I found myself flying backwards as the feedback hit me. Didn't expect that. I hit the far wall and actually saw stars. A couple of my newly-healed bones broke again, adding to the cacophony of pain.

I got to my feet and whirled to face him, intent on ending this as quickly as possible. He had scrambled back toward one of the cabinets behind him, keeping his right hand tucked tightly to his body. I was dismayed to see that he still clutched the dagger, but now that he was hurt, I figured it was only a matter of time before I got it away from him. Ward or no ward, I've done this before. I crept towards him, dimming myself as I moved.

Bress didn't waste time talking. He yanked open the door of the cabinet and pulled out an automatic handgun with an extra-long magazine sticking out of the bottom. I knew he could empty it in just a few seconds, that is, unless he was smart enough to only fire a few shots at a time. Of course, he was. He started firing short bursts, forcing me to dodge and weave as I approached. He was surprisingly accurate, missing me by only inches each time, and I realized that he must have been able to see me in spite of my glamour. One of his shots clipped me in the kneecap, and the pain was truly impressive. I skirted the summoning circle on the floor and dived behind the granite altar. Its aura immediately started working on me, making me sick to my stomach, but I ignored it as best I could.

"You're quite resourceful," Bress snapped, anger and pain coloring his voice. He kept the gun trained on my position. I simply waited. It would take a while before my knee was right again. Even so, I had to find a way to take him out.

His voice echoed from the marble floor and bounced around the room. "What are you, really? I thought you were just an adventurer with some talent, but I was obviously wrong."

"Just a soldier trying to keep the balance, Bress," I countered. "You're nothing but another bad guy. I'm here to take you out of the game."

He fired a quick burst that made me duck a little as the bullets pinged off the dark granite of the altar. "Bigger players than you have tried," he sputtered. I could hear him fumbling with something. He seemed to be having trouble with it. In any case, it wouldn't do for me to give him too much time to regroup. Kneecap or no kneecap, I had to make a move.

I looked over to where the cables had fallen once I had broken apart their enchantment. Now, they were nothing more than inert metal ropes. Ordinarily, I might not be able to do much with them, but they were also covered in my blood. That allowed me some leeway.

Reaching out with my magick, I touched the cables. They rebelled at first, but my blood overpowered the reluctance of the steel. I exerted my will, which took far more energy than I liked, but things were getting dicey. It was worth a shot. I poured my power into the enchantment I'd created, visualized the effect I needed, and the cables rose from the floor like steel cobras. I took a deep breath and sent them whipping violently towards the corner where Bress was holed up. I heard him yell in surprise, and that's when I whirled and vaulted the altar, fangs and teeth ready to rip him apart.

Man, I really thought that would work.

Chapter 26

Ariana and Maximus burst through a pair of doors and found themselves in a new hallway that led left and right. Without hesitation, Ariana chose the corridor to her right, and pulled Max along beside her. They passed a number of closed glass doors, but a glance told them that those offices had no other exits and were nothing more than cells, fancy cubicles for Bress's workers. They quickly reached the end of the hallway and ran right into another set of double doors. They went through only to be confronted by a wall with a sign, arrows pointing down the hallways that stretched away to either side. One of the notations on the sign got Ariana's attention.

"Come on!" she urged Max as she took the right hand way. He gamely stumbled along beside her, somewhat less clumsily than before. The exercise seemed to be doing him some good, though he was still extremely weak, and the collar was still keeping him from recovering as he might. Even so, he managed to match her pace.

They reached another, bigger set of glass doors, and she quickly swiped her card in front of the reader, which beeped merrily to allow her access. She yanked open the doors and helped Max over the threshold. Ariana looked around and whistled. "I guess Bress wants his employees to stay fit," she mused aloud.

They had entered the corporate gym. Everything was stainless steel, black rubber, and firm, gray carpet. The smell of sweat was faint, overpowered as it was by the pine and lemon smell of the cleaners the maintenance staff used. They faced an enormous circular reception desk, and beyond that, they could see several rows of weight machines. Ariana's eyes darted around the darkened facility, seeing by the light of the few fixtures that were permanently on. She scanned the racquetball courts and group fitness rooms off to her left, and then the free weight and cross training areas on her right. Any other time, she might have been impressed with the array of equipment, but she had no time for that as she looked for a way out. Finally, she spotted what she was looking for on the opposite side of the room and bolted around the big desk, Max trotting alongside her.

"I assume you have a plan of some kind?" Max asked, still struggling to keep his breathing even.

"Yes," Ariana answered simply. "I just need to get us outside of the building and buy us a few minutes to get out of here. If what I saw online about this place is correct, I think I know of a way."

"Couldn't we just shoot out a window?" Max suggested.

"We could, but that would tell them where we are right away. They know we're on this floor, but that's it. Besides, I have a way to get us down, I think, and it won't work if we go out a window. Just trust me."

On the far side of the room was a wide stairway that doubled back on itself once as it led to the upper floor of the gym. Their feet pattered on the stairs as they made their way up. Just as they reached the top, Ariana heard a muffled beep from somewhere behind them. Someone had swiped a keycard across the reader at the front. A moment later, she felt a distant rumbling through the soles of her boots as a small herd of feet suddenly clambered into the gym below them. Rather than the terse commands of the security guards she expected, she instead heard bestial growls and snarls, and she realized that the goblins had apparently found another way up.

"Dammit," she cursed softly as she helped the king over the top step. "I was hoping for just a few more minutes." She looked around and found the sign she was looking for. The smell of chlorine was already thick in her nostrils, and her eyes followed the arrow on the wall plaque that told her where to go. She pointed so the king saw it too. "Max, head to the pool. I'm going to try to slow these guys down, but I'll be right behind you." Ariana slipped him the keycard as she spoke.

"The pool?" Max could not imagine why they would go there, but took the keycard and quickly headed in that direction. Moments later, the lock beeped open, and he was through the doors.

"Now, let me see what I've got in here..." Ariana knelt, whipped off her backpack and unzipped it in practiced motions. The noise below was soon followed by a horrid stench as the smell of the goblins wafted up the stairs. "Oh, ugh." She made a face, but kept digging in her pack until she found what she wanted.

Staying low to keep out of sight, Ariana crept halfway back down the first flight of stairs, then peeked over the low wall to see what was going on. Her eyes widened at the sight.

A troop of thirty hideous, snarling goblins were swarming the gym. She had seen a goblin before, but that had been a long time ago, and she had never dreamed she would see so many in one place. The door slammed at the far end of the gym, and a man stood there, wearing the same tactical equipment the other security guards had worn. His AR-15 was held at the ready. Even from that distance, Ariana could see that his eyes were wide with fear. He did not like this job, but seemed determined to see it through.

"Gob One is in the gym," he spoke aloud, his voice echoing in Ariana's stolen earpiece. "Search underway, will report."

"Gotcha, Gob One," came the reply. "Hey, make sure you send a cleaning crew in there when you're done, Collin. Y'all stink." There was clipped laughter on the other end before the communication was cut short, and Ariana heard Collin swear. She shook her head, then turned her attention back to the creatures that were hunting for her.

Their skin was a dark, mottled green, and their eyes blazed red. All wore dirty leather armor and carried wicked looking daggers and short swords. Many had black, stringy hair while others appeared to be shaved. Some even had black, bristly mohawks. Multiple earrings dangled from long, pointed ears, and their noses jutted out from gnarled, angry faces. Sharp fangs gleamed in overly wide mouths. They were squatty, but strongly built. While she watched, one of them picked up a barbell someone had left out and casually tossed it aside with one three-fingered hand. Her eyes widened as she recognized that the bumper plates on that bar had easily totaled two hundred pounds. They snarled and hissed as they searched the gym, entering every fitness room and office. One bulled through the daycare area, scattering and breaking toys as it went. Ariana's eyes narrowed at that. She liked kids.

"OK, creeps," she muttered, "let's see how you like *this*." Leaning back as far as she could on the stairs, she raised the small slingshot she had found in her pack, pulling the ammo pouch to the anchor point on her chin. She sighted on one of the automatic sprinklers in the ceiling on the far side of the room and released her hold on the small leather pouch, sending its cargo zipping through the air over the heads of the goblins. The small ball of hardened gelatin struck the ceiling just in front of the sprinkler head, erupting into a sticky goo that covered the device. "Yes!" Ariana whispered to herself. She quickly put the slingshot away and pulled out a tiny lighter, then slipped her arms back through the straps on her backpack, readying herself to flee.

Narrowing her focus, Ariana quietly chanted the words to the spell, holding the lighter in her left hand and gesturing carefully with her right. A soft glow appeared around her right hand as she finished her chant, and she quickly flicked the lighter, causing a flame to spring to life. She grabbed it with her right hand, capturing it as though it were a fluttering moth, and held it as she gathered her will. The tiny fire needed to stay alive for just a few, precious seconds. With a flick of her wrist, she sent the flame shooting across the empty space toward the sticky fuel she had deposited on the distant sprinkler head. The instant the fire hit the fuel, it exploded in flames, triggering the sprinklers throughout the entire gym.

Water ferociously cascaded down from the ceiling in sheets, drenching the goblins below. Their furious howls made Ariana smile as she wiped the water from her face. As quickly as she dared, she scrambled up the stairs and crawled toward the doors that Max held open for her. He was grinning widely.

"Goblins don't like water very much," he observed.

"I know!"

Chapter 27

Of all the things I might have expected him to throw at me right then, I was totally unprepared for what I saw when I leapt over that altar.

Nothing. Bress was supposed to be right there, fighting off the cables I had just sent his way, but he was gone. The steel cables whipped the space where he had been, lashing deep gouges into the wall behind, but then they flopped to the floor, their energy spent. I pulled up short, carefully eying the corner where Bress had been just moments before. The handgun lay on the floor, a faint wisp of smoke rising from its barrel. In the walls, I saw no seam, no door, no other way out. For the moment, his escape was a mystery.

I narrowed my eyes and mentally shifted my gaze until the auras became visible. The natural energy of the objects in the room glowed with various colors, some faint, some intensely strong. I could see the ugly, scarlet aura shining from the altar at my back without even turning around. Keeping my claws ready, I began to turn in a slow circle, searching for Bress. He couldn't have gotten far in so little time. Even if he had a killer veil, I could still find him. I'm sure my eyes glowed in the shadows of the room as my magick awakened. Bress was close, and I wanted a piece of him.

There, I thought. I caught the shine of crimson energy that shouldn't have been there. Whatever was giving off that glow was behind the desk on my left, just below my line of sight. *The dagger,* I thought. How he'd managed to get from the corner to that hiding place was beyond me, but that really didn't matter. What mattered was getting my claws into him as quickly as possible.

I sprinted over to the desk and rounded the corner only to find the dagger lying on the floor. No Bress. I scooped it up, knowing that I couldn't use it on anyone, not even Bress. The last thing I wanted to do was feed energy into whatever spell he was creating. Suddenly, I felt a disturbance in the air. I turned around and saw him standing on the opposite side of the room, grinning hugely, though sweat was rolling down his face.

"That was a nice move," I offered. It had been. Evading me in such close quarters was no mean feat.

"Thanks," he grunted. He smoothed his hair and straightened his tie, but was visibly winded. "Portals are strenuous, but useful."

Ah, that's how he did it. Bress was proving to be a much stronger magick user than I had anticipated. Portals were incredibly difficult, not to mention dangerous. He could have emerged right in the middle of the altar instead of standing next to it. Most humans don't have that kind of control, nor do they have the sheer strength of will and body to survive going through one. I doubted Bress would be able to do it again so soon, but unfortunately, he didn't need to. I couldn't get to him easily now, and there was an open doorway behind him. He could bolt at any moment.

"You're no adventurer. Who are you?" His shiny green eyes glinted as he stared at me across the summoning circle. He was smart enough to keep it between us, since we both knew he could use it to trap me. His heart was beating fast, and he was struggling to look like the portal hadn't just exhausted him. "A man with your talents, I might have a job for you. Are you for hire? I can definitely make it worth your while."

He was stalling. I knew it, and he knew I knew it. I looked off to my left and saw the switch that opened the door that led out into the office. It was only a few feet away.

I had a choice before me. I could escape to come back another time, healed, well-rested, and knowing his capabilities. I had the dagger. It might not be a bad idea to get it as far from him as possible so that it couldn't be used to finish his ritual. I brought my eyes back to his as I thought about my other option, which was to fling myself at him, regardless of the risks, and rip his heart out. Bress met my stare with a wolfish, hungry look at first, but when I didn't look away, it slipped a bit. Beneath his carefully cultivated arrogance was a growing sense of uncertainty. He wasn't used to having to work this hard, and it was eroding his confidence. I grinned and finally let my fangs show, keeping the rest of the Bress mirage intact around my body. As I had hoped, that unnerved him further.

"No thanks," I said, and burst into a leap that took me to the marble wall on my left. I hit it with my left foot and immediately sprang off it towards

Bress, my claws reaching for him as I flew through the air.

As I came off the wall, he threw something in the air between us, and I flew face-first into a cloud of white-hot, flaring particles that sparked and thundered as arcs of energy jumped across its widening field of influence. The bastard had lightning dust. All I could do was cover my face, tuck, and roll through it. Small, but powerful lightning bolts ripped into me as I passed through the cloud. I landed hard on my right shoulder, and pain shot through me again. I tried to recover, but Bress stepped in and kicked me in the face. Hard. Bress apparently doesn't miss leg day.

I staggered back, cursing my weakness. I had kept the dagger in hand, but barely. It had become a hindrance. I thought about sticking it in my tactical vest, but that was too dangerous, and I had to handle this hand to hand. And Bress would do anything to prevent that from happening.

He slapped a hand on a panel near the other door in the chamber and the door slid open, spilling a faint, flickering light into the chamber. "Get him, you idiots! And chain him to the altar! I want him to fuel the ritual!"

Three huge men rumbled past Bress on their way to reach me, and I knew I was in for a fight. Each carried a riot baton, and one sported a pair of brass knuckles. Although they shared similar suits, bald heads, and vacant stares, these guys made Lars and Knut look like midget wrestlers. Easily seven feet tall and three hundred pounds of muscle on the hoof apiece, they nevertheless moved like professional athletes. I wondered for an instant why he had Knut and Lars around when he could have used these guys, then I noticed that each wore a thick metal collar similar to what Maximus had worn. The symbols inscribed on each collar were glowing with a dim scarlet light that was mirrored in their eyes, and I realized that the collars weren't suppressing their powers as Max's collar had been. These were channeling power *into* these guys, drawing energy from another realm, and not a land of sunshine and butterflies, either. Bress had been a very bad boy, messing about in dark magicks that should really have been left forgotten. No wonder the Goddess sent me after him. Maybe she should have done it a little sooner. Ah, well, that's her business, I just do the dirty work.

"And get that dagger away from him! I need it!" Bress commanded. He seemed to be regaining his composure, though he still looked a bit green around the gills.

The three men walked right through the casting circle, and I saw their collars flare as they crossed the lines. *Interesting,* I thought. I made a mental note to look into Bress's conjurings more closely when this was all over. He was doing some very innovative things with his magick. It's a shame he was a bad guy.

I needed both hands free to deal with the stooges, so I stepped back and flicked the dagger toward the high ceiling. It stuck and quivered there for a moment before falling still. Satisfied that it was out of reach for the moment, I turned my attention to the three advancing behemoths. I slipped my claws out all the way before realizing that their throats were solidly protected by the collars. *Damn,* I thought. I left my claws out anyway. *Time to earn my pay.* I flung myself forward to meet them and it...was...ON.

Chapter 28

The pool door closed behind Ariana and Max, shutting off the maddened cries of the goblins in the gym below. Water wouldn't harm them, but they hated the feel of it on their skin, and they were throwing an impressive tantrum while their human overseer desperately tried to get them back under control. Ariana looked out over the indoor pool and whistled softly.

"Ok, that's impressive," she whispered, her voice muffled by the falling water. Even though the steady rain from the sprinklers overhead obscured her view somewhat, she could still see that Bress had spared no expense in building the company pool. Several lanes for lap swimming were closest to them, plus an enormous Jacuzzi nearby. Where the pool opened into a larger swimming area, the surroundings had been made to look like a tropical beach resort, with stone landscaping and palm trees carefully placed around an open bungalow. As much as Ariana would have enjoyed exploring the grand space, she focused on the task at hand. "Over there!" Rather than explain, she took Maximus by the arm and ushered him around the pool until they reached the massive windows that faced the outside. Through the windows, Ariana confirmed that the pool continued under the glass wall into a wide balcony, also decorated as if it were a tropical lagoon. "We're wet already. We can get out through here, and I think I can get you down from the balcony."

"There's a gate down there," Max offered. Where the pool passed under the wall, connecting it with the outdoor section, a gate of stainless steel bars was locked in place.

"Not for long," Ariana answered. She had already spotted the control panel, hidden behind a faux rock formation. She flipped open the panel and pushed the button. A distant whirring sound confirmed that she had turned something on. "Is it moving?"

"Yes!" Excitement colored his voice. "The gate is going down!"

Ariana craned her neck and looked into the water, enjoying the burst of triumph she felt at seeing the bars retreating into the bottom of the pool. "Quick! Swim under the wall and I'll follow you. Head for that palm tree out there." She pointed to an area on the balcony outside where a large palm tree would shelter them from their pursuers.

Maximus slipped into the water and quickly swam under the wall, angling towards the nearest set of steps in the outdoor pool. Ariana followed moments later. They emerged from the water into the cool night air, stunned by the sudden silence as they left the noise of the furious fall of water from the sprinklers behind.

Ariana smoothed her wet hair out of her face as she helped Maximus up the steps. Soft night lights illuminated the luxurious outdoor pool, but left plenty of shadows for the pair. They moved behind the huge potted palm tree, where they knelt and looked out over the street below. The skyscraper across from them was far too distant, its facing too smooth, for them to consider. Ariana bent and peered through the railings to see the street six stories down.

Whipping off her pack, she turned wide eyes towards her charge. "So," she began excitedly, "have you ever done any rappelling?" Her quick hands pulled a coil of rope from its depths that looked far too big to have fit in the bag in the first place, especially with an AR-15 shorty and ammo, plus whatever else she had packed inside originally.

Max's golden eyes looked at her in surprise. "What all do you have in there?" He leaned over to peek inside, but he could see nothing inside her backpack.

She hurriedly zipped it closed. "Lots of things," she replied, somewhat abruptly. "I wish I'd have put more in it, to be honest." She shouldered it again and began to uncoil the rope. "So...rappelling? Have you ever done it?"

Max turned his attention back to her and nodded. "I have. I spent some time in South Africa, and my...colleagues...insisted that I learn."

Ariana played out the rope and wrapped it around the base of one of the fence railings, a thick post that felt sufficiently sturdy. After carefully checking to see that they were unobserved from below, she tossed both ends of the rope over the railing. They fell short of the ground, but not terribly so, and she judged it safe enough.

"Here, let me get you set up. We've got to get you out of here, like right now!" She had him stand as she pulled up a few yards of rope and crossed them behind his back. Then she had him step over the two lengths and brought the ropes together between his legs so they came out behind him. She then pulled the two lengths together and wrapped them around his right forearm. "OK, this is not going to be comfortable, sorry. Just let it out here, like this," she demonstrated, "and get yourself down as fast as you can. I'll come down right behind you." She paused for a moment, then reached into a pocket in the side of the backpack and pulled out a key dangling from a small chunk of granite as a keychain. These, she tucked into the left leg of his tights where they would stay secure. "Next time, I'll bring some extra clothes with pockets. Look, if I don't make it down, get to my Jeep. It's in the parking lot around the corner that way," she pointed. "My address is on the insurance card in the glove compartment. The house is warded. You'll be safe there, I guarantee it."

"Warded? You're a witch?" Max asked, not sounding entirely surprised. "How do I pass the ward?"

"Yep, I'm a witch, and a damned good one if I may say so. The keychain is also a key to the ward. Just keep it close to your body and it'll let you pass through, you don't have to do anything else. You ready?"

Max tested the arrangement of the ropes, and nodded. "Yes, this feels familiar enough that I think I can do it." Without further ado, he climbed carefully over the railing and leaned back into the makeshift rope harness. He turned his head and looked at the unforgiving pavement far below. Even if he fell from this height, it wouldn't kill him. It would break him, though. He'd be helpless for quite a while. And it would hurt. Max smiled to himself at the thought. *At this point, I'm no stranger to hurt, but I'll avoid what I can.* He turned his attention back to the young woman who was putting her life on the line for him. "Hurry down," he said quietly.

Ariana grinned. "I will if you ever get your butt moving, Max."

Maximus nodded and leaned farther back. He carefully let the pair of ropes slide through his right hand as he began walking down the side of the building. Ariana had been correct: the ropes burned his arm and back, but the arrangement worked. He began to pick up speed as he remembered his former skill. Every so often, he looked up to see Ariana's face directly above him, her expression urgent, but encouraging. Reminding himself to look around for security guards, he walked his way down to the ends of the rope, which left only a slight drop to the sidewalk.

He extracted himself from the arrangement as he reached the bottom, dangled as low as he could, and then let go of the ropes to land unharmed on the concrete. He looked up to the balcony above.

"Ariana!" he whispered as loudly as he felt was prudent. "I'm down! Come on! Ariana!"

Silence was the only answer. Ariana was nowhere to be seen. His heart sank.

Maximus called up to her a few more times, and when it was clear that there would be no answer, he cursed softly and loped in the direction of the parking lot Ariana had mentioned, keeping to the shadows as best he could. He was still weak, still a shell of the man and beast he should have been. Escape did not feel like any kind of victory.

Chapter 29

The first thing to remember when fighting more than one attacker is that you need to keep moving. If you let them surround you, you're going to pay for it. You need to move around in such a way that the bad guys can't come at you all at once. Sidestep a lot and make them have to climb over each other to get to you. That way, you only have to fight one at a time. Generally, I'm fast enough that I can just go right in the middle of a crowd and kill anything that gets near me, but after the beating I'd already taken, I figured it was time to be smart for a change.

The brute nearest me took a swing with his riot baton, and I dodged it. As the motion carried his arm past me, I darted forward and grabbed it, then spun so that his momentum did the heavy lifting for me. I sent him slamming into the number two guy a few steps behind and heard a satisfying crunch as the two butted heads. They went down in a heap, but number three simply leaped over them and came at me swinging.

He was quicker than the first had been. The baton moved in his hand like a whip rather than a club, and after dodging his first swing, the speed of his return stroke almost caught me. It glanced from my shoulder as I tried to slip it, knocking me off balance. That wasn't so bad, but the punch he landed to my chest with his brass knuckles...OK, that hurt. Reflexively, I dug all of my claws into his punching arm as I fell away from him. He hurt me, yes, but I ripped that arm to bloody ribbons in the process. Unless he could heal as fast as I, he wouldn't use it on me again. I flew back into the wall, and the impact knocked the wind out of me. Number Three wasn't screaming in agony, but he had dropped his baton and was holding his maimed arm close to his body, so I knew he felt it. Although the pain in my chest was making it hard to breathe, I had to press my attack. I leaped forward, grabbed the baton he had dropped, then shattered his right kneecap with it. He toppled to the floor, grunting in pain as he hit. I kicked him solidly in the head for good measure, and all the fight went out of him. One down, two to go.

That's when Number One grabbed me from behind. He wrapped those enormous arms around me and picked me up off the floor, squeezing me hard enough that I thought my eyes would pop out. My hands were pinned by my sides. I struggled to get my hands around in front of me so I could attack his arms, but that wasn't happening. I slammed my head back, trying to headbutt him, but he was too big, and I only hit him in the chest. I kicked my legs and tried to hit his knees, his groin, anything, but he shrugged it all off. I was stuck.

Meanwhile, Number Two was on his feet again. He shook his head to clear it, then his beady, red eyes fastened on me. What might have passed for a smile appeared on his bloody face. He pulled a black fabric bag out of his pocket. Moving faster than I expected, he slapped it over my head and yanked the drawstring tight around my neck. I was blind.

Great. Just great.

Number One grunted and carried me over to the altar. I felt Number Two grab my ankles, and in spite of my frantic kicking, he managed to get my left leg strapped in securely. Working together, they got me on the altar, strapped in my other leg, and then started working on my arms. I went limp for a moment when they tried to get my left wrist buckled in, then lashed out again. The sudden movement freed my arm just long enough for me to cause trouble. I felt my claws slide through flesh and felt a hot splash of blood on my arm before they caught it again and brutally slammed it down against the cold granite. My head was pressed against the stone and I tried to bite through the bag. That only got my head slammed back down, and hard. That dazed me a little, and when I came back, I was strapped in tightly. I was going nowhere.

The bag was ripped from my head just in time for me to see Number Two collapse, blood gushing from his neck just above the protective steel collar. Number One stood impassively by, his eyes vacant. Bress stood next to the altar to my right, still standing a few feet away just in case I happened to get an arm free. I grinned.

"What's the matter, Bress?" I said, "You nervous?"

His green eyes glittered with malice as he stared at me. He had regained most of his composure, though he was still breathing heavily. "Nervous? No, not nervous. Curious, though, definitely. Even through all that, your veil is still in place. You still look like me. That takes not only power, but skill and control. You don't learn that after only a handful of years of training." He shook his head slightly, but continued smiling. He was on to something, and he knew it. "Whatever you are, I'm thinking that you'll do nicely for my sacrifice. The girl was specified because of her power, but one of the Fae?" He smiled, "Yes, that's what I think you are. One of the Faerie would do nicely."

I closed my eyes and began chanting in a pained whisper.

"Hm? What's that?"

I kept going, whispering just a bit louder. I tried to weave a suggestion into the words, urging him forward, urging him to *want* to hear me. He leaned closer to hear...and stopped before he got too close. Straightening up to his full height, he chuckled. "Nice try. No way am I getting that close to your teeth. You definitely seem like the biting type." Bress turned to the remaining thug and nodded towards the two enormous bodies on the ground. "Get those idiots out of my sight, and then," he flicked a glance at the dagger I'd stuck in the ceiling. It was far out of reach, even for the apish arms of Number One. Bress rolled his eyes. "Then get a ladder and get that damned dagger down from there. Let's get this over with."

Chapter 30

Ariana watched King Maximus work his way down the wall, pleased that he seemed to be moving well. She saw him look up at her briefly before turning his attention back to his task. When she was sure that he would make it down safely, she turned away. She took a couple of running steps and dove into the pool, angling her dive so that she came up inside the building. The sprinklers were still running, and although the noise of the falling water was still loud in her ears, she was thankful for it, knowing that it would hide her from the goblins below. She swam smoothly to the side and pushed herself up and out of the water, then moved in a crouch over to one of the windows that looked out over the exercise area below.

Ariana's eyes widened as she saw the mess the goblins had made. Equipment was scattered everywhere, mirrors were broken into wicked shards, and everything was in total disarray. The goblins were still pretty pissed off by the incessant fall of water from the sprinklers, and worked off their anger by brawling, howling, and tearing up whatever they got their gnarled hands on.

Their keeper yelled and used a short whip to get their attention, but the water hampered his efforts. As she watched, one of the enraged goblins charged him. Though his eyes were wild, he dropped the whip and raised his gun, expertly putting two holes in the creature's misshapen forehead. However uncertain the man had seemed at first, he was a still professional killer. The sound of gunfire was muted by the artificial rainfall, but it apparently got their attention. Their frantic thrashing and wrestling slowed. The man yelled something Ariana could not make out, then shot another pair of them that had refused to stop battering each other. Finally, the goblins began to settle down. One by one, then in larger groups, they all turned to face him, listening at last to his commands.

Ariana realized that this was not helpful for her situation at all. To make matters worse, the water that had been hiding her movements abruptly stopped flowing from the sprinklers in the ceiling, leaving a silence that was almost deafening by contrast.

"Crap," Ariana muttered. She saw the guard's eyes flick in her direction once. He turned to the nearest goblins and began to speak. Then he stopped and turned his full attention towards her. His eyes narrowed as he tried to decide if he had seen what he thought he had. Ariana ducked out of sight below the window. "And double crap."

She was moving before she heard the guard order the goblins up the stairs to investigate, but she felt their heavy feet thumping as they approached.

Staying low, she hurriedly made her way around the swimming pool to a service door. She grabbed for the keycard, but then saw that the door had no control panel, just an ordinary lock. Suddenly thankful for the time her uncle had spent teaching her about locks when she had been younger, she knelt and pulled a set of picks from her vest. The lock clicked open in under a minute, and she quickly let herself inside, trying not to think about the goblins stampeding up the stairs and banging on the glass windows of the pool area behind her.

Once inside, she relocked the door and flipped on the lights. It was a supply closet, and a big one. Rows of heavy-duty shelving lined the walls, and the smell of chlorine was thick in the air. A quick inspection showed that there was no other door, and Ariana cursed. Suddenly, the door behind her rattled, and she heard the grunting language of the goblins as they argued about the fact that it wouldn't open. She immediately looked up and saw a standard suspended ceiling with white, rectangular panels hung in a grid overhead.

She knew she would be leaving wet footprints, but she could do nothing about that. Speed was more important. She tested one of the rows of shelving at its end and found it to be more than sturdy enough to hold her weight. Staying close to the wall, she used the shelves as a ladder and climbed up to the ceiling. There, she pressed one of the tiles up and out of place, then moved it aside so she could get through. Moving as carefully as she could, she climbed up and stuck her head through the hole she had made and saw what she had expected. The suspended ceiling masked a rougher ceiling a few feet overhead. More importantly, it allowed her access to the next room behind the supply closet, a room that was not part of the gym complex. The space was just high enough to leave room for her to crawl along the top of the wall next to her. She slipped her arms out of the straps of her backpack and pushed it up through the hole, carefully resting it on top of the wall, then climbed up into the ceiling after it. She settled herself, balancing carefully, and reached for the ceiling tile to replace it. Then she stopped. She could clearly see her wet footprints on the floor below. The goblins would be inside in moments, and they would certainly see them and find her. She had to distract them, just long enough to let those prints dry.

Ariana fished a tiny plastic bag from a pocket in her cargo pants and opened the zipper seal. She carefully shook a small, tissue wrapped bundle from the bag and held it carefully in her palm while she put the baggie away. Shutting out the noise from below, she brought her mind into focus, gathering her intent and pouring it into the little lump in her palm. When it felt right, she flexed her will and released her power. The blob in her hand glowed a bright blue in response. When it began to make a soft buzzing sound, she dropped it down into the room below, then replaced the ceiling tile.

The door to the supply room slammed open, and a goblin stepped through the doorway. It was met by a loud bang, immediately followed by a billowing cloud of bright blue smoke. The goblin yelped in surprise and fell back into its fellows, who had crowded in the door right behind him.

"Come on, come on, what's the problem?"

The leader shoved the nearest goblins aside and looked into the supply room, still filled with the thick, roiling smoke. "Dammit, what happened in here?" He pulled his sidearm and aimed it into the room, searching for a target. "Freeze!" he yelled. When he received no answer, he popped off five rounds anyway, then waited.

A minute passed, then the smoke began to clear. Thirty more seconds and it dissipated, leaving nothing but a silent supply room. At the far end, the state of the art washers and dryers now sported bullet holes and broken glass.

A voice crackled in Collin's ear, "Report."

Collin sighed. "Negative. She was here, though. The Sec-Bot was trashed, and she blocked the doors in a couple places. She triggered the sprinklers in the gym, but there's no fire up here." He paused, his mind racing. "She set off a smoke bomb or something in the supply room by the pool, but that was likely a distraction. She must have gone out somewhere else. We've searched the entire area, she's gone now."

There was a long beat of silence before his earpiece came alive again. "Fall back to second floor and await further instructions."

"Affirmative," Collin sighed. The goblins were milling around in the pool area behind him, taking care not to get too close to the water. He looked into the supply room one last time, but saw nothing amiss other than the bullet holes he had left. Shaking his head, he turned and left the room, letting the door swing shut behind him. "It's gonna be a long night," he muttered.

Chapter 31

Bress had changed out of his suit and into a black, loose-fitting pair of Japanese silk pants and a pair of black slippers, leaving his upper torso bare. For the first time, I could see all the scars he had inflicted upon himself in the pursuit of the power he now commanded. He was covered with them. From the looks of it, he'd started young, and kept at it. I had seen that kind of thing before, but most people like Bress were far too vain to mutilate themselves so extensively. The fact that he was willing to go that far definitely revealed something about his character. Mostly that he was thoroughly insane. Humans willing to perform the kinds of rituals that necessitated such scarring were often a lot of trouble for someone in my line of work. As he had already proven, that was quite true in this case.

"Admiring my work, are you?" He said, sounding absurdly smug. He traced one manicured fingernail over one of the sigils on his right bicep. "Yes, each one was quite painful, but absolutely necessary to get me where I am today. They were worth every moment of agony. Those pains are long gone, but my power remains."

I raised an eyebrow, and received a mirror image of the same expression from the man himself.

"You know it's not really *your* power," I said. "You're just borrowing it. The pain from those scars is barely a down payment. One day, you'll have to pay off the remaining balance, now won't you?" I grinned at him. This time, he did not return the favor. Instead, his brows furrowed, and a glint of anger had come into his eyes. I kept prodding, "I've seen what happens when the Dark Ones come to collect, and let me tell you...the interest is gonna hurt."

He backhanded me. I was expecting it. I wasn't even mad.

"Once I finish this ritual, that won't happen for centuries, if at all!" he barked. "And in the meantime, I'll extend my reach all over the world. I'll be more wealthy and powerful than someone like you could ever dream."

"Sure, Bress. Whatever you say," my Bress-voice dripped with sarcasm. "You just go right on thinking that. You'll end up as a toy for something hideous, wait and see. That's how you all end up. All that power and money will count for nothing in the end, and that's what you'll be: nothing." I enjoyed seeing his face flush a bit more, but that satisfaction was fleeting. I was still the one shackled to an altar and due to be sacrificed soon. I tried to think of a way out, but I had to admit, I was stumped at the moment. If I could keep him talking, then I at least had a bit more time to come up with something.

"I think I've had enough of your commentary," Bress announced. He snapped his fingers at the gorilla that had just returned from disposing of his comrades. When he had the brute's attention, he pointed at my face. "Shut him up."

Uh oh.

The big guy nodded and went over to the desk in the corner. He opened a drawer and pulled out an odd-looking contraption, a flat piece of leather with straps on either side and a short rubber cylinder sticking out of its center. As I watched him approach, I felt the cold of a gun barrel being pressed to my temple. I cut my eyes back to Bress to see him holding the gun, grinning widely.

"You're fast, but even you can't dodge a bullet from here. Now stay still, or I'll just kill you now and wait for the girl."

Oh, I was so looking forward to killing him. I just wasn't yet sure how I was going to do it. I sighed and stayed still as the big guy put the elaborate gag in place. He pressed the leather pad over my mouth so that the rubber piece jammed between my teeth, then strapped it all tightly around my head. So much for being able to distract Bress with conversation.

At this point, I was hoping that the Goddess would give me a clue. I've been in rough spots before, and on rare occasion, I've received a powerful and timely flash of insight that kept me from certain death. I'd long since learned not to depend on them, trusting in my own talents and skills to get me out of such scrapes on my own, but I was beginning to think that I would need one if I was going to get out of this. I flexed against the leather and steel straps that held me, but they held fast. I'd have to get through straps on my biceps, wrists, thighs, ankles, and torso before I would be free. As much as I hated to admit it, things weren't looking good.

"There now," Bress purred, "the rest of the ceremony can continue without the benefit of your unnecessary input." He placed both hands on the altar and leaned over to look at me. "Yes, I like you this way much better. I think we are almost ready." His eyes flicked to the desk across the room, and saw the open box that laid there. Remembering that the dagger was now embedded in the ceiling high overhead, he glanced in that direction, and grunted in frustration. To the goon, he said, "Didn't I tell you to get a ladder and retrieve that dagger? What are you waiting for? Get moving, you idiot!"

Oblivious to the harassment, the big guy simply turned and pressed the button next to the sliding door. His expression never changed from one of bored disinterest. As the door slid open, he disappeared through it, dutifully heading out to find a ladder.

"Now we wait," Bress said. He walked over to the main panel and touched an icon. Classical music filled the room, wafting from hidden speakers. "Don't worry, you won't have to wait long. And your death will be painless. Almost."

I cut my eyes over to the dagger I had embedded into the ceiling. Unless I could figure something out in a hurry, I knew I was looking at the instrument of my death. As much as I hated to admit it, I was beginning to think that there was going to be a job opening in my field before too long.

Bress moved over to the control panel and began tapping icons. I felt a mechanism engage somewhere in the floor beneath the altar, and the whole thing started moving. By painfully craning my neck to one side, I saw a big section of the conjuring circle slide away. Floor panels moved aside to allow room for the altar to slide into position. Once the altar reached its destination, the panels reorganized themselves so that the circle was complete again with my heart at its center. Not a good sign for me.

Bress tapped another icon. "Lars? Is he there?"

There was a long pause before the reply came. "No, Mr. Bress. The door was locked, but he is no longer in his cell."

Rather than cursing, as I expected, Bress simply closed his eyes and took a slow, calming breath. Then he cut his eyes towards me and glared murder for a few seconds before turning back to the display. "All right then, he's telling the truth. Go and secure the other asset, just to be safe, then come back here. Leave the other intruder to security."

"You mean...*that* asset, sir?" An unexpected note of uncertainty crept into Lars' metallic voice.

Bress tapped the icon angrily, "Yes, you idiot! That one! Under no circumstances does she escape. Understood?" He paused, and then lowered his voice almost to a whisper I'm sure he thought I couldn't hear. "In fact, prep her for transfer. Release the demons guarding her, and have her moved to site B immediately."

The response was quick, and Lars was all business once more, regardless of his personal feelings. "Yes, sir. I'm on it."

"You'd better be, you moron!" Bress tapped the icon again and turned off the intercom. "Idiots!" he fumed. With some effort, he regained his composure. He even managed to smile at me again. Oh joy.

"Now then, where were we?" He made a show of tapping his chin with one finger as if trying to remember. "Ah, yes! I was about to sacrifice you to Shar-Nakhan so that I can live forever! That is, once I get that dagger down from where you deposited it."

Just then, the door opened to admit Number One. He was carrying a ladder that looked absurdly tiny for him. Without comment, he opened the ladder and set it up underneath the dagger. I could hear the metal creaking beneath his weight as he climbed up the thing, but it held him long enough that he was able to dislodge the dagger from the ceiling. If he was relieved to have his feet firmly back on the floor, he didn't show it. He walked over to Bress and handed him the dagger before stowing the ladder away in a corner of the room. His short list of tasks completed, he took up a station outside the conjuring circle and simply stood there, waiting, his red eyes glinting in the dim light of the room.

Bress walked over to the area of the circle I knew was its northern quadrant, and grasped the dagger in both hands. Without looking at him, Bress admonished his guard, "Stay out of the circle once I begin." The big man simply nodded. Bress looked over at me, bound and gagged on the black granite altar, and he smiled again. "You've been quite a thorn in my side tonight, whoever you are. At least, in death, you'll be of use to me."

Holding the dagger in his right hand, he uttered a few harsh syllables, and candles at various points along the outer edge of the circle suddenly ignited, bright yellow flames erupting spontaneously from their wicks. Then Bress hummed a low, bass note, deep in his chest. He did it again, louder. I could feel the energy building already. I strained against my bonds, but they were industrial strength leather and steel, and I was held fast. Bress began a low, ugly chant.

The air over my head suddenly looked odd to me. As I watched, it began to gather itself, to take on substance, as if the shadows in the room were suddenly multiplying and joining together to form something tangible. The darkness began to spin, slowly moving into a steady spiral, glinting with hints of scarlet and ugly yellow as Bress's will began to coalesce. His voice began to rise, and along with it, a distant rumble. This sound had nothing to do with machinery beneath the floor. No, it rose from a much more distant place. Echoes of ancient evil rose from the abyss, and a bone-deep feeling of dread made my blood run cold. I struggled again, biting at the piece of rubber in my mouth, but only a muffled grunt emerged, unheard in the rising noise.

The golden lines in the floor began to glow scarlet as the spell began to take hold. A wind from another dimension arose, a foul and hateful gale that tasted of sulfur and brimstone. It ruffled Bress's hair and plucked at Number One's jacket and tie. The rumbling became louder as Bress's chanting grew stronger, and the bloody light shone brightly from below.

Bress took the dagger in a two-handed grip, pointing the blade downward at my heart, and he slowly approached the altar, blood and lust showing in his eyes of bottle-green.

It was not a good day.

Chapter 32

Ariana pushed open the door to the supply closet she had entered by way of the ceiling, and carefully peeked outside. She was back on the sixth floor, and the door opened on another hallway lined with small offices. All was quiet for the moment. When she heard nothing from either direction, she eased through the door and gently closed it before heading down the hall to her left. Her sense of direction had always been good, and now, as she navigated the warren of cubicles and conference rooms, she was grateful for it.

Two different times, she was forced to hide as more Sec-Bots went about their rounds, but she was prepared for them, and they passed without incident. It took her a few minutes to find the elevators that would take her back up to where she had left Kane. She knew Kane had told her to escort Max to safety, but the growing feeling of dread in the pit of her stomach told her otherwise. She had long ago learned to trust her gut, and it was practically yelling at her this time. Whether it was women's intuition or that of a witch, she was compelled to listen and act on it.

She pressed the elevator button, and felt the mechanism engage from deep within the building. She knew that there was a better than average chance the elevator would be occupied, but at this point, she had no choice. She rested her hand on one of her pistols, but left it holstered. Instead, she reached up and pulled a small expanding baton from where it attached to her backpack. With a flick of her wrist, she whipped it open, and then stepped away from the doors of the elevator so she would not be in plain sight when they opened. Using the same strategy as she had before, she grabbed another stone from a nearby planter. Then she waited.

With a cheerful ping, the elevator doors slid open, but there was no sound from within. Ariana arced the stone up and over the open doorway, and it clattered noisily on the tile floor opposite her. Holding her baton at the ready, she pressed herself against the wall next to the door and waited.

A half second later, a burly man in a guard uniform poked his head out of the door, looking in the direction of the sound. He had his gun in his hand, held in a good shooter's grip, but pointed at the ground. The guard glanced to his left, and when he saw nothing that could have made the noise, he started to swing his gaze to the right. Ariana neatly clubbed him in the back of the head before he could register her presence, and he dropped heavily to the floor, unconscious.

Looking at the strongly built man on the floor, Ariana shook her head. "Geez, do they get all you guys from the same farm or something? What a bunch of thugs!" After propping the elevator door open with her baton, she dragged his limp form behind the planter, and gagged and zip tied him as quickly as she could. That accomplished, she retrieved her baton on her way into the elevator and pressed the top button on the panel. The doors slid shut, and Ariana made herself take a deep breath. It would only take a minute or so for the elevator to reach the floor below Bress's penthouse suite, but there were more than twenty floors full of guards she had to pass before she would get there. Any one of those guards could see the elevator moving and decide to push the button. Suddenly, all of Kane's talk of climbing the elevator shafts made a lot more sense.

Fortunately, she made it to the top floor unmolested, and the doors opened on the richly furnished foyer where the guard known as the Gatekeeper had been sitting. The big desk remained empty, much to Ariana's relief. She strolled across the marble floor and used the keycard to open the lock on the frosted glass door, admitting her to the plush waiting area.

She made her way across the room, casting a quick glance off to one side to be sure that her boyfriend was still sleeping soundly behind the couch. He was still there, snoring softly. She shook her head and smiled. *I need a guy like that,* she mused, *but smarter. And he needs to like musicals.*

Still musing, she passed the door that led to Max's former prison, and she approached the big wooden doors where the white-coated man had gone. Fortunately, the doors were unlocked, and she had no trouble getting inside. Ahead, she saw another hallway that led to what she guessed was Bress's private elevator, flanked on either side by stairwell doors. She took the leftmost, and headed up the stairs to the penthouse suite.

She listened carefully at the door when she reached the top landing, and heard a faint mumbling and scuffing sound. After a few seconds, she decided to chance it and take a look. When she opened the door, she saw two more guards on the floor. They were alive, but thoroughly pissed off.

And it was hilarious.

"I hope neither of you had burritos for lunch," she whispered.

The two men had been gagged and then secured in a most embarrassing arrangement, each man's face buried deeply in the other's crotch. Kane had immobilized them so thoroughly that there was no chance they would escape until someone found them and cut their bonds. They couldn't even look up at her. They were trying to yell behind their gags, but only muffled noises emerged, and the pair of them wiggled around like an enormous worm.

She repressed the urge to burst into laughter, but just barely, and left the two frustrated men writhing on the floor behind her as she moved into the penthouse suite.

Her boots made little noise as she made her way across the marble floor, and she stuck to the thick carpet where she could. The artwork on the walls would ordinarily have caused her to stop and stare, but she ignored the paintings as she approached the fountain in the center of the chamber. *Impressive,* she thought. Looking past the fountain, she saw the wide balcony, left open to the starry night. She scanned it until she was satisfied that it was deserted, then she focused her attention on what looked like Bress's personal office, a huge space dominated by a desk and surrounded by elegant bookcases and leather furniture, all enclosed behind a wall of glass off to her left.

Before she could move towards it, she heard another door open somewhere out of her line of sight. She sprinted past the fountain and onto the darkened balcony. Ducking into the shadows, she flattened herself against the wall. Moving as slowly and carefully as she could, she peered around the corner.

Her eyes widened as one of the biggest men she had ever seen walked into view carrying a step ladder. It almost looked like a toy in his enormous hands. A thick, silver collar surrounded his neck, and his eyes glinted scarlet when the light hit them.

"Holy King Kong, Batman," she whispered to herself.

The brute walked over to the doors in the glass wall and let himself inside the office. He took two steps and then stopped. He took a breath as if to speak, but only stood with his mouth open for a couple of seconds before closing it again. A perplexed look appeared on his face, and one of his big hands came up to cup his chin as he apparently tried to remember something. He gently laid the ladder at his feet, and then began to search his pockets.

Ariana knew an opportunity when she saw one. Sticking to the shadows, she eased back inside the building and moved as close to the office as she could without bringing attention to herself. When she was almost close enough to touch the nearest glass wall of the office, the guard pulled a piece of paper from his pocket and opened it up.

In rumbling, bass voice, the guard began to read from the paper. Ariana recognized the words as an old German chant, a kind of key that would open a ward spell. She paid close attention to the words, as German was not her best subject. She watched the guard hold both hands high and make three quick gestures with his fingers as he finished the chant. There was a flash from inside the room, and Ariana saw the outlines of the formerly invisible ward that had been in place in the office. Ariana's eyes widened at the sight of it; a ward that thick would pack a serious kick, maybe even enough to take down a creature like Kane.

The guard picked up the ladder and stepped closer to the desk. He turned back around and read from the paper again, a shorter series of German words, and there was another flash as the ward went back up. Satisfied, the big man picked up the ladder again, and walked over to one of the bookcases. He pushed a button, and the bookcase slid open to reveal a hidden door. The guard disappeared inside, and the bookcase closed behind him.

The moment the bookcase stopped moving, Ariana bolted to the office. She carefully opened the glass door, and stopped just as the guard had, only a couple of steps in. She cast her senses throughout the room, but found no trace of the ward. She shook her head, admitting that Bress knew his stuff where wards were concerned. She couldn't find it anywhere. She took a deep breath to clear her mind, then raised her hands and repeated the words she had heard the guard say moments before, punctuating the last syllables with the same three gestures.

She grinned as the ward flashed brightly and turned itself off. "Take that, you ass," she said, pleased that she had sidestepped his defenses again.

She checked both her handguns to be sure they were fully loaded, then she eased towards the bookcase, flipping the office lights off as she went. *No sense in giving them a brightly lit target before I see what's in there,* she thought. She had a strong feeling that things were about to get interesting. Her fingers traced the smooth wood of the shelves until she found the button. She took a deep breath, then pushed it.

The bookcase slid noiselessly open, and a bright crimson light spilled out from the chamber beyond, accompanied by a foul gale that smelled of the underworld. A loud chanting had begun, and the very sound of it made Ariana's head hurt and her stomach clench as her body rebelled against words that should never have been spoken aloud. Steeling herself against the vile energy that came pouring out of the room, Ariana pulled her other handgun from its holster. Thus armed, she pressed forward.

Chapter 33

This was it. End of the road. Bress stood less than a foot away from me, gripping a sacrificial dagger in both hands, chanting his ass off, and I couldn't do a thing about it. The dagger's tip was hovering a few inches over my heart, and I knew what was next on the program. Even though the shackles had already proven their sturdiness, I strained against them anyway, definitely not willing to go gentle into that good night, dammit.

Bress stared down at me, triumph in his eyes and a nasty grin on his face. As his chant neared its end, he raised the dagger over his head.

That's when the shooting started. Three shots rang out, pop-pop-pop, and Number One toppled over on his face like a fallen redwood. His enormous form fell across the glowing circle on the floor, breaking the spell Bress had created, and sending a powerful blast of magickal feedback into the sorcerer. He grunted in agony as he tried to disperse the dark energies that threatened to tear him apart even as he stared in disbelief at Number One's body. A figure emerged from the darkness with two guns held ready. One booted foot rested on the goon's back as if claiming it.

It was Ariana. I had never been so happy to see a human in my life. She stood there, blond hair dripping wet, an avenging angel with a gun in each hand and a grim smile on her face. Both of those guns were trained on Elias Bress, and she was pissed.

"Drop it, Bress!" she yelled.

The disruption of his spell had hit him hard, and he was struggling just to stay on his feet. The ritual was done, broken, and his chance for near-immortality had just passed him by. He'd lost. He stared at Ariana uncomprehendingly for just a beat, then his eyes found mine. I actually saw his sanity crack wide open in that moment, and whatever control he had just vanished. Bress uttered a primal cry of rage, and staggered forward, determined to kill me and gain at least that much satisfaction. He hurled himself at me with the dagger held high, and in his haste, he tripped over his own feet. Lucky bastard, that's probably all that saved him. Ariana's next shot struck him squarely in the back of his right hand, blowing a good-sized hole in the meat. He screamed in agony, and the knife clattered to the floor. Bress ducked behind the safety of the black granite altar as Ariana threw a few more shots his way. I hoped she was being careful not to hit me, then I realized I still looked like Bress. Instinctively, I dropped the veil, momentarily revealing my true self before I got it together and shifted my appearance to the one Ariana recognized. Beside me, Bress gasped. Dammit, he'd seen. In a voice thick with insane glee, he hissed in triumph.

"Ah, *there* you are! I see you, GrimFaerie!" I turned my head and stared into the cut-glass green of his eyes, now bloodshot and crazed with agony. "I know what you are now." He chuckled crazily as his mind latched onto a new plan of action. "This isn't over. I'll find you! And the girl, too. When we meet again, you'll end up begging me to kill you both!" Oh, yeah, he'd definitely gone off the deep end. But staring into those crazy, burning eyes, I saw into him much farther than I might have wanted to, and what I saw unnerved me.

Ariana fired again, and Bress finally retreated. He clutched his ruined hand to his chest and scrabbled his way backwards like a crab, being careful to keep the altar between himself and Ariana. He scuttled over to one wall and reached as high as he could to slap a button. A panel slid open, revealing a narrow set of stairs leading upwards. Bress crawled up the first few steps, and the door snapped shut behind him, leaving us in silence.

Chapter 34

"Kane?" Ariana asked, keeping her guns aimed at the wall where Bress disappeared.

"M hmm mm hmm," I said, eloquent as always. I shrugged my shoulders at her as best I could. *Would you mind getting me off of this bloody thing?*

Upon hearing my voice in her mind, Ariana moved quickly to my side, holstering her guns as she did so. "Kane!" she said, both relief and concern filling her voice as she looked over my shackled body. There was still a lot of blood from Lars and Knut's playtime. "What...how in the hell...?"

Again, if you could just get me off of here, I'd appreciate it.

"Sorry, sorry," she said. She reached behind my head and unbuckled the straps on the gag. When she pulled it away, I sucked in a big double-lungful of air and then worked my jaw a couple of times. "Are you all right?"

"I'm fine," I grunted, lying through my teeth. "Get me loose, we've got to catch him!"

Between the two of us, we unbuckled the straps and freed me from the altar. My legs were shakier than I cared to admit, but I didn't have time for their weakness so I just ignored it.

I caught my balance and together we hurried over to the wall where we had seen Bress disappear. We found the mechanism that opened the hidden door and pressed it. The panel slid open to reveal the cold concrete stairs. I took the lead, Ariana following close behind. I noticed the splotches of blood on the stairs, and grinned. *At least she hurt him,* I thought. *Bastard deserves much worse, but at least he'll have a hard time working spells with that hand now.*

We worked our way up to the next landing, a plain concrete affair with a simple security door labeled Roof Access. Outside, we could hear the loud whup-whup-whup of a helicopter's blades, and I knew that we were too late. I laid into the door with my shoulder and it slammed open, admitting a fierce gale that confirmed what I already knew.

A black helicopter was leaving the helipad, almost lazily lifting its runners from the surface of the roof. I caught a glimpse of Bress's bloody face as he glared at me through a panel of safety glass in the passenger compartment. Suddenly, the glass between us cracked in a star pattern as Ariana tried to put a bullet into Bress's head, and the copter veered jerkily away from us. It wobbled, then turned northward, showing us its tail rotors. The pilot gave it some gas and the helicopter sped away, its flight smoothing out as it gained speed. It dodged the nearest of the towering buildings and we lost sight of it amidst the cityscape. The overpowering sound of the copter's rotors faded away, leaving nothing but the wind blowing around us.

"Well, crap," I heard Ariana mutter behind me. I turned to see her holster her gun, then blow a stray lock of hair from her eyes. "I'll say this for him, he's a slippery devil." She looked at me again, this time examining me from head to toe and back. "Are you all right?" she asked again.

I considered the question for a moment before answering. It had been an unusually rough night, even for me. Many of my bones had been broken, some repeatedly. Thanks to my natural resilience, they had healed up already. They were sore, though, and mightily so. And hitting the ward in Bress's office had taken a ton out of me. I needed some food and some rest in a way I hadn't in a long, long time.

"I will be, yes." Then I realized that she wasn't supposed to be there at all. Alarmed, I asked, "Wait, where's King Maximus? Shouldn't you be with him?"

"I got him to the ground and gave him the keys to the Jeep. He should be safe at my house by now. I gave him a keystone so the ward wouldn't get him." Ariana looked around the roof and up at the starry sky, admiring the view and enjoying the momentary peace afforded us by the night. She sighed, "Sure is pretty up there."

I looked up and let my eyes rove over the heavens above. Although I saw a great many things with my Fae sight that she could not, I knew that what she was seeing was still quite beautiful. "It is, I agree. Let's get back inside. I have some unfinished business in there."

We followed the stairs back down to the conjuring room and I saw what I was after. The dagger lay on the floor next to the altar, and I walked over and picked it up. No way was I leaving it lying around for anyone else to find. I hated the oily feeling of the handle. I'm not a squeamish sort, but this thing...it was bad. Fortunately, I had seen Bress take the dagger from a wooden box on his desk, so I took the blade over there. A quick examination revealed runes that I easily recognized, and the warding spells were simple enough. I laid the dagger in the bottom of the box and closed it up. A wave of my hand and a few archaic syllables engaged the spells and sealed the box in a flash of golden light. I picked up the box, relieved that I wouldn't have to touch the dagger again. I'd get it to my elders for safekeeping, and hopefully, they'd actually hang on to it this time. To Ariana, I said, "Is there room in your pack for this?"

In answer, she whipped off the pack and unzipped it. "You bet," she answered confidently. "Give it." She reached out a hand to accept the box and then quickly stuffed it out of sight inside. When she reshouldered the pack, I raised an eyebrow.

"Exactly how big is that thing inside?" Her pack had looked only half-full before, but even with the bulky wooden box added, it still looked the same.

A wry smile quirked one corner of her mouth. "It's bigger than it looks. What now?"

"We've got to get out of here and see to the king. He needs our help."

"It won't be easy," Ariana admitted. "The place down there is swarming with goblins and security," she paused for a moment, "and other stuff we haven't run up against yet, I'm sure."

Just then, she froze as if listening. One hand absently reached up to touch the earpiece in her left ear.

"What is it?" I said.

She cursed, then shook her head. "Bress just radioed security from his helicopter. They're on their way up with everything they've got."

I swore, though I didn't have enough energy to put much heat into it. Ordinarily, I love a good battle. It's something I'm good at, and I generally find such things invigorating. At that moment, however, I was thinking that taking on the entire building's security forces, both supernatural and mundane, was going to be a bit much even for both of us. I sighed, trying to come up with a plan that did not end with us dying under a swarm of goblins or riddled with bullets.

As if to make the point, there was a vague rumbling noise outside the conjuring room. I felt it through my feet more than I heard it, but I knew exactly what it was: everyone else in the building was gathering outside Bress's office, planning their assault. Then there was yelling as their officers directed traffic, getting everyone into position. The sound that really made my day was the deep, groaning bellow of a troll. This one sounded alive, as well as cranky. This was not likely to go well.

Ariana's eyes suddenly widened in surprise. "What the...? Hang on." Sounding startled, Ariana interrupted my less-than-optimistic musings. She reached into a pocket of her cargo pants and pulled out a cell-phone encased in a sturdy rubber shell.

She swiped at the screen and stared at it for a moment. One of these days, I might have to get one, but so far, I was stubbornly refusing to do so.

"I hope you had that thing off. It would have been bad for it to have made noise back there somewhere."

"I had it on silent, it shouldn't even have vibrated, but it did. I just got a text from Maximus."

OK, that surprised me. "Wait, what?"

Ariana shook her head in disbelief. "I don't even know how he found my number, much less activated my phone. It says to go to the roof. Like right now."

The hidden door to Bress's office slid open and three smoke grenades came flying into the room. I snagged two of them before they hit the floor and chucked them right back out again, following them up with the third one immediately afterward. The surprised yells I got in response made me smile as I pushed the button to close the door again. *Let them chew on that for a bit.* I turned back to Ariana only to find her already on the stairs, gesturing wildly at me.

"What are you waiting for, let's move!"

I was only too happy to comply. We raced up the stairs to the roof and again heard the distinctive sound of helicopter blades above us. When we broke through the roof access door for the second time, the wind nearly blew us right back inside.

The copter that awaited us was a sleek black job, emblazoned with a stylized wolfs head logo on the side, along with Lucanis Enterprises written on the tail in an elegant script. The doors were open wide and the pilot, a stern and sturdy looking young man, was standing next to it with an AR-15 slung across his back. He bowed to us rather formally, gestured quickly to the open door, then unslung the rifle and focused his attention on the roof's exit. We wasted no time in climbing aboard the copter and getting buckled in. The moment we were securely inside, the pilot quickly closed the big door behind us, slipped into the cockpit, and expertly lifted us off the roof. In seconds, we left the Bress Building far below. It had already faded into the dark behind us when we finally got the headsets on.

"Welcome aboard, Miss Ariana...Mr. Kane," the pilot's voice sounded tinny in our ears, but even so, there was reassurance in his tone, along with a note of amusement. "My name's E.J. Simmons, but you can call me Edge. I've been sent to collect you both and take you to your home, ma'am. Mr. Max is awaiting you there."

"He's safe?" Ariana asked, concern in her voice.

"Yes ma'am, he contacted us while en route to your place. He's there now, resting and awaiting your arrival." There was a pause, and I saw him turn to look over his shoulder at us. His teeth gleamed in the moonlight as he grinned. "It's not my place to say, ma'am, but there's a better than average chance that he's eaten everything in your fridge by now."

Ariana made a scoffing noise. "He's welcome to it. I hope he enjoys the meatloaf."

The pilot turned back to the front, still smiling. "Oh, you can count on that. Yes ma'am. Both of you can just relax and enjoy the ride, I'll have you back home in short order."

Ariana leaned back in her seat and folded her arms, smiling as she looked out over the lights of Houston as we flew westward. I said nothing. I'd already taken the pilots advice to relax, and it's hard to talk when you're asleep.

Chapter 35

As the sky began to brighten, heralding the approaching dawn, the helicopter landed in one of the open fields on Ariana's property. Responding to the pilot's expert touch on the controls, the big machine touched down as gently as a hummingbird. Edge shut down the machine, ditched his helmet, and brought out his AR-15 before escorting us to the house. He carried it with quiet authority and kept a careful eye on the predawn sky above, watching for anything that might pose a threat. He seemed like a pretty stalwart fellow, this Edge Simmons, and I liked him. The fact that he worked for King Maximus also reflected well. Max had always been known to attract good people.

We followed a narrow path through the woods and emerged near the old barn that served as a garage. Ariana was relieved to see that the Jeep had been parked in its proper spot. As we approached the porch, Edge stopped just short of the house ward.

When Ariana saw that he wasn't following, she apologized and took his hand to guide him through the invisible barrier. He said nothing, but a faint grin appeared on his face at the touch of her hand.

"Thank you, ma'am. I could feel it there, and something told me that I didn't want to walk into anything you'd put up for security purposes. Mr. Max warned me to be careful."

"You could feel it?" Ariana raised an eyebrow. She wasn't used to normals being able to recognize magickal workings.

He nodded. "Yes ma'am. I've had some training. All of Mr. Max's top people have."

Ariana looked like she was about to say something more when the screen door opened on her porch. Maximus emerged from within the house, smiling and looking much steadier than he had when I'd last seen him. He was drying his hair with a big blue towel and wearing a red bathrobe that was far too small for him. The silver torque was still around his neck, but his golden eyes crinkled at the edges as he smiled at the three of us.

"Well met, my friends! I am beyond pleased to see you all safe." To Ariana, he bowed slightly. "My lady, I must apologize, but I was famished upon my arrival. I feasted on the remains of your meatloaf, as well as a few other things. I am sorry to have left your proverbial cupboards bare."

Ariana laughed and glanced at Edge to share their joke, only to find him down on one knee, his head bowed reverently. Before she could speak, Maximus addressed the man.

"Mr. Simmons, as always, I find myself thanking you for your service. I knew I could count on you."

"Thank you, Your Majesty," Edge replied, keeping his eyes downcast. The respect in his voice was deep and sincere. It said far more about Max than it did about Edge, and I felt glad that there were a few truly honorable beings in this world. Max was, indeed, one of the good ones. "It was my honor to assist."

Maximus came down the steps and put a hand on the man's shoulder. "Rise, young sir. And thank you again." Edge returned to an upright position, obviously pleased at the praise. To Ariana and me, the king said, "Shall we retire indoors? I am still rather weak, and I would love to be rid of this damnable collar if at all possible."

Ariana brightened immediately and bolted up the steps to her front door. "I think I have just the thing! I've got to get the spells off it, of course..." She disappeared inside the house for a moment before returning to hold the door open for us, an impatient look on her face. "Well? Come on!"

We all looked at each other and smiled as we followed the witch into her house. While Ariana and Edge went to work on the collar, I found a couple of protein bars and washed them down with water. I felt like I could have eaten a horse, but since none were available, I figured a bigger meal would have to wait. I listened to Ariana chattering away at Maximus, answering his questions and explaining how we had come to find him, and I chimed in here and there to clarify. I was happy to let her do the talking so I could keep eating.

Once the infernal rumbling in my belly had been dealt with, I let myself out the front door again. I walked into the woods, following the same path I had taken before we had left to assault Bress's tower. The forest closed around me, surrounding me with its primal energy, and I found myself relaxing at last. As before, I let my mind wander and my feet followed after. Soon enough, I found myself in the same part of the woods I had seen twice before. I entered the rough circle of taller trees and arranged myself on the ground. I released the glamour that hid my true form and gently sent out a call.

Tatyana, I said in my mind, willing my words to echo silently throughout the forest. I conjured the image of the tiny Sprite in my mind, allowing the sight of her beauty to guide me, and I called her again. *Tatyana, I have news.*

Almost immediately, I heard the high-pitched tinkling of Faerie bells, and a wee ball of light appeared in the branches of the trees over my head. I was pleased to note that the bells sounded much stronger than the last time I heard them. The glowing sphere drifted down in front of me until it was close enough to touch the ground. Then it vanished, leaving the gorgeous little Pixie standing there, her dragonfly wings iridescent in the moonlight. Her wounds had healed, and she stood proudly, displaying her comely form in all its tiny glory.

She raised her chin haughtily and met my gaze. "Grim," she greeted me curtly, a thinly veiled challenge woven into her words. "Why have you come?"

I surprised her by bowing, placing my hands on the ground before me and lowering my forehead to them before sitting up once more. She eyed me warily, and then curtseyed in return.

"We have met the man who did you harm, Elias Bress, in battle."

"He is dead, then?" Tatyana asked calmly.

"Sadly, he is not," I replied. Her brows furrowed in disappointment at my words. I continued, "However, we hurt him deeply. His right hand was mangled by the witch's bullets. We stole his dagger of summoning, and helped King Maximus Lucanis Von Gerhardt escape from Bress's prison."

Tatyana's face brightened immediately and her wings buzzed with excitement, lifting her into the air until she was hovering at my eye level.

"That, Grim, *is* wonderful news! The loss of his hand will surely rankle, and the thought of his suffering is most pleasing. The king is known to us, the news of his release is also cause for joy. He has always been most honorable in his dealings with our kind, few though they may be." She gazed at me with her glowing Faerie eyes, and then cocked her head in confusion. "As much as this news is welcome, why are you here? Our deal was complete. We had no further bargain."

"I..." I began, then stopped. My reasons for being there felt decidedly unFaerie. Nevertheless, I pressed forward. "I agree, there was no further bargain, implied or otherwise. I owe you nothing." I sighed. "Nevertheless, it was my wish to share with you this news in the hopes it would brighten your hearts. I was saddened that you and your people were injured in keeping our bargain."

Tatyana looked at me for a few moments. Then she smiled. "That is unusually kind for one such as you. Your gesture will be remembered. Although of course, no favor is owed." She winked at me and then shot skyward in a burst of light and tinkling bells.

I watched her go, still wondering why I had bothered to come out here. I'm not a sentimental sort, and there was truly nothing to be gained from my visit. Even so, something within me felt better for having made the effort. Shaking my head at my own foolishness, I rose and headed back to the house.

*   *   *   *   *

"Hold on...almost got it...there!"

The king was sitting in one of Ariana's kitchen chairs, naked to the waist, while she worked a large pair of bolt cutters in an attempt to break open the collar. It had taken the better part of an hour for Ariana to dismantle the defensive spells built into the collar, but finally, it parted with a loud snap and a bright flash of light.

Maximus sighed with relief, then gripped the ends of the metal circlet with both hands. With surprising strength, he bent the thick metal collar outward until the opening was wide enough for him to lift it away from his neck and over his head. He brought it in front of him and stared at it, hefting its weight in his hands. He shook his head slowly.

"I can't tell you how pleased I am to be free of this infernal device." He lifted his golden eyes to Ariana, who still held the bolt cutters in both hands.

"You have my heartfelt thanks and undying gratitude." He handed it to her, and she took it. "Since you've removed the enchantments on it, maybe you can melt it down into something more useful."

"You can count on that, Max," Ariana replied. "I can add it to the mix when I make my next round of reloads. Who knows, I might even get a chance to give it back to Bress someday, one bullet at a time." She stood and left the kitchen for the conjuring room, intent on stashing the straightened collar. Moments later, she returned and sat in one of the kitchen chairs. "Now then, where do we go from here?"

Maximus was silent. He had closed his eyes when Ariana had gone and had yet to reopen them. He slowly rolled his head from side to side, as if limbering it up, and sighed deeply. He rolled his shoulders forward and backward, then stood up and stepped away from the kitchen table so that he had room to move. As we watched, his body began to change. His shoulders thickened before our eyes as his muscles regenerated, throwing off months of magickal suppression. His chest filled out and the ropy muscles of his arms swelled until they resembled those of an aging powerlifter. A grunt escaped him as his legs expanded, the wasted muscles repairing themselves. He began to growl low in his throat, the power of it rattling the glasses on the table. He hunched over and clenched his fists as his body suffered the agony of coming back to its natural state, free at last from the shackles of

Bress's magick. Finally, he sighed, the sound much deeper than before. He rose to his full height, his golden eyes glittering, a faint smile on his face. He was magnificent.

"Edge," Maximus rumbled, "you brought my clothes?"

"Of course, Your Majesty." Edge bowed, then handed over the metal case he had fetched from the helicopter.

"If you will all excuse me, I'd like to make myself more presentable. And Edge, if you would be so kind as to procure some food for us all?" Arrangements were made, and Edge left with the keys to Ariana's Jeep while Maximus retired to the guest bathroom to dress and compose himself. When he returned, the transformation was astonishing.

The man we had first met as a hunched, trembling, and frail prisoner, covered with blood and grime, his hair and beard matted and greasy, was gone. In his place stood a tall, ferociously handsome man of middle years, erect of posture and wide of shoulder, moving with the smoothness of a wild animal only recently cultured. His dark hair had been swept back to reveal a rugged face dominated by deep-set golden eyes and flashing white teeth. His dark blue suit had obviously been tailored for him, and the fine fabric was set off by an elegant purple tie and handkerchief. He pulled a chair out so he could face all of us at once, and then sat down, somehow making the simple wooden chair seem more like a throne.

"Wow," Ariana finally managed.

The king laughed - a hearty, full-bodied, and jolly sound. "Yes, I usually prefer to take better care of myself. My imprisonment left me in a regrettably shabby state, especially with that collar. It suppressed my body's natural vitality and healing abilities, and so my muscles practically withered away. Without the collar, my body was free to renew itself properly." He turned to Ariana and me, smiling broadly. "Again, I cannot thank you both enough. From today forward, you will have access to any help I can provide you. My resources are," he chuckled a bit before continuing, "rather extensive. Whatever your needs, you have but to name them. I will leave you the means to contact me directly. When you call, I or my people will come to your aid."

I spoke up. "Bress is still out there. We stopped him from performing this ritual, but once he recovers, he's sure to cause trouble again. He's completely mad."

"Indeed he is," Maximus agreed. "I will have my people put on alert. His business interests can run without him almost indefinitely, but he'll have to surface somewhere. When he does, I'll find out about it. As distasteful as I might find it, I'll need to see that he's dealt with so that he has little chance to hurt others in the future."

Ariana spoke up, "Do you think he'll come back here?"

Maximus shook his head. "That's doubtful, at least for the foreseeable future. He's much more likely to hole up somewhere and have everything he needs transferred covertly to his new location, put some distance between you. He'll think you're planning to come after him, since that's what he'd do."

"We should," Ariana said, her frustration coming to the surface. "He had all those other girls killed. I'm sure the law won't catch up with him. We should take him down once and for all."

"Patience, Ariana," Max said, his voice low and calming. "His day will come. I'll find him eventually, and that will be the end of it. He made a mistake in abducting me. I have the means to make his life miserable, and then eliminate him." He sighed and shook his head. "I hate that it comes to that, but his actions warrant no other response. He's dangerous, and must be put down. When I do find him, you'll be notified immediately."

That seemed to satisfy Ariana for the time being. She looked over at me. "What about you? Are you going to try to find him?"

I shook my head. "No, my place is here. I go where I'm sent, and until I hear differently, this is my territory. I'll stay until the Goddess tells me otherwise."

"I wish every city had a GrimFaerie," the king said, nodding in my direction. "There would be a lot less trouble from evil men like Elias Bress."

"I'm sure there would still be plenty to keep them all occupied," I said, knowing that every Grim I knew was frightfully busy, just as I was. Evil seemed to be everywhere these days.

Just then, Edge walked back in the door, carrying several white bags with an orange logo on the front, all heavily loaded. The smell of breakfast tacos and biscuit sandwiches made my stomach twist in knots of delightful anticipation. He tossed the keys with the ward keystone to Ariana, then laid the bags on the table. "I hope I brought enough," he said.

Maximus growled before he caught himself. His golden eyes glinted with hunger and he smiled a frighteningly predatory smile. Then he laughed. "I hope so, too."

We all dug in as if we hadn't eaten in a month.

*   *   *   *   *

The sun was shining down on a beautiful day, and Edge throttled up the engine on the helicopter. The blades began their circular spin, and the breeze began to pick up. We were far enough away that we could still hear each other easily, but that would change in moments.

Maximus stood tall and proud, relishing the feel of the sun's warmth on his skin as he savored a deep lungful of country air. He turned those golden eyes on Ariana, and I felt her heartbeat quicken as his attention fell on her. His was steady as a rock.

"I must say," he began, "I wish it had been under better circumstances, but I'm awfully glad we met."

Ariana met his gaze evenly, a faint smile touching her lips. "Me too, Max. It was fun."

He grinned, showing even white teeth, and laughed. "You know, it's been many years since I've been called anything but 'sir,' or 'Your Majesty.' No one calls me Max but you," he raised an eyebrow. "I think I like it."

Before she could respond, the king of the werewolves produced a thick envelope from his jacket pocket and held it up. "I've got a couple of my company credit cards in here. I figure you might need financial backing, especially if Bress stirs up trouble again. Don't worry about the limits, there are none. There's cash in there too, it has its uses as well." He paused, and I sensed his pulse accelerate. Not much, just enough that I noticed. He continued, "There are also two phones programmed with my direct numbers." His eyes stayed locked on hers. "In case you need me."

He handed over the envelope, and she accepted it. I noticed that one of his fingers touched hers for a moment longer than was probably necessary. She didn't seem to mind. I resisted the urge to roll my eyes. Although she was far from my type, Ariana was attractive, capable, and smart...for a human. It wasn't surprising that Maximus had taken a liking to her.

He turned to me and offered his hand. I took it, and returned his firm grip with my own. Every fiber of his being was giving off a sense of gratitude and respect. Although I usually could have cared less, his was one opinion that meant something to me.

"And Kane," he rumbled, "if there's ever anything you need from me, you just name it."

I laughed. "You should know better than to bargain with one of the Faerie, Your Majesty," I suggested.

He shook his head, and he gave me a knowing smile. "No bargain was ever struck. But even so, I don't forget such things. Ever. Thank you."

"You're quite welcome, Your Majesty." I offered a slight bow, which he returned.

With another radiant smile at Ariana, he turned and headed for the chopper.

When he was buckled in the passenger seat, he waved at us, and Ariana and I waved back. Edge lifted the copter off the ground and we watched it rise a ways before it leaned forward and put on a burst of speed. It flew northward, towards Dallas and one of the king's business headquarters. Ariana kept her eyes on the helicopter until it finally disappeared in the distance. Then she shook her head slightly and let out a low whistle.

"He likes you," I said simply.

She turned and quirked an eyebrow at me. "You think so?"

"Indeed," I said. "He probably wants to mate with you."

Ariana's mouth dropped open and she looked at me, aghast. Then she rolled her eyes. "Wow, that's romantic," she said as she turned and started walking toward the house, flustered. "He should be so lucky. It'll take more than a buttload of money, and being big, strong, and handsome to get me to, uh, *mate* with some random guy."

I fell in step beside her. I didn't understand her embarrassment, but humans still befuddle me now and then. So many hangups. I figured the best course of action would just be to agree with her. "Right," I said. "Of course." And somehow, I felt relief. I'd have to examine that feeling later...it didn't make a lot of sense. Oh well. It had been a rough couple of days.

We reached the house and went inside. Shaking off her confusion, Ariana dropped the packet on a side table. Then she walked over to where she had deposited her guns and backpack when we had arrived hours earlier. She picked everything up, and spread it out on the kitchen tabletop. She cast a glance over her shoulder at me, then explained somewhat gruffly, "I need to get my stuff put away and my guns cleaned." Then she softened, "Otherwise, it makes me itch, you know?"

"Sure," I said simply, and she went back to her work while I sat down in one of the chairs nearby. "Do you mind if I stay here until dark?"

"That's fine, you can rest in the guest room if you like."

"Thanks, I'll just relax here for a bit if that's ok."

"Yeah, sure," she said without looking up. She was involved in her task now, pulling things out of her backpack and arranging them on the table. There was a surprising number of items, and they just kept coming. The short-barreled AR-15 really got my attention, especially since I knew it shouldn't have fit in there in the first place. When she was finished, I was one hundred percent certain that all of that could not have fit inside the backpack she'd been wearing all night. *Witches and their tricks,* I thought. I almost smiled.

Without looking up, she addressed me again. "Well, Kane? Now what?"

Before answering, I sat and thought about the events of the previous night. One thing had been bothering me for some time, and I finally had to acknowledge it: the vision the Goddess had shown me had not come to pass. Ariana and I had never encountered the group of demons I had seen. In my long experience, that just didn't happen; if I saw a vision, it always came true. Always. That only left one explanation.

I sighed as I realized that the vision I had been given must still be somewhere in my future. Our future. That meant I was stuck with her. I glanced over at Ariana and watched her as she organized the supplies on the table. Some of the implements I recognized as spell components, while others were far more difficult for me to identify, in spite of my long experience. I admit that I'd never have pegged the snow globe as being capable of felling two lesser demons as it had, so no matter how innocuous the items in her pack, I had to consider that they might be pretty potent. The fact that four knives, an expandable baton, a slingshot, and a blowgun also went on the table did not escape me. In fact, it finally did wring a smile out of me.

She set the empty pack down, moved over a bit, and started in on her weapons. She started humming a little tune as she field stripped the first of her handguns. I watched her fingers flitting over the cold metal, so sure in their movements, and I realized that having her around might not be such a bad thing after all.

"Hey," she said. I realized that she was looking at me over her shoulder and had caught me staring. "What are you looking at?"

"Nothing," I replied simply. "Just admiring your efficiency."

She shrugged and went back to her work, but I noticed the small smile that turned up one corner of her mouth. "So like I said, what now?"

"I guess we'll just have to wait and see. The Goddess tells me what I need to do." I paused to take a breath before continuing. "I have a strong feeling I could use some help. You're good in a fight, and you know the world I live in. Interested?"

I heard her heartbeat quicken with excitement. Her voice, though, was calm, almost dismissive. "Maybe," she offered. "I have been getting bored around here lately." She shrugged. "Sure, why not? Might be fun."

I agreed. It might, at that.

Chapter 36

The entity known as Shar-Nakhan coiled and seethed, screaming in rage, though no sound was heard in the icy dark of the abyss. For all its plotting and planning, its schemes had been ruined, its unknowing champion maimed and incapacitated.

That Grim! And that witch! it screamed, its words unheard and unfelt by any mortals, though any mortal would have instantly died under the power of the thing's fury. *They dare to hinder me!*

It had been so close, so incredibly close to breaking through. The pathetic human, Bress, had thought he would gain immortality through his ritual. In truth, he would have only opened the door to his own demise. One more life would have sufficed, one more heart pierced by one of the ancient daggers, and the way would have been clear. Now, the heavens had moved out of alignment. Another way must be found.

Bah! it shrieked in the cold and dark. *I will yet triumph! I will find a way! Then there will be nothing but the wailing of souls as an entire world dies in horror to feed my essence.*

That thought comforted the ancient presence. Indeed, it finally began to see where its next move would be, where it had to be. Through a slender crack between worlds, it reached out, sending the tiniest piece of its own awareness into the human domain. It sought what it knew best; sorrow, fear, rage, and despair. In a place almost as dark as its own, it found what it sought. A being, human, but not entirely so. It was strong, and yet its spirit was weak and malleable. It was of the light, but tainted by the shadows in which it had thrown itself. And so a new plan was made. And then, the ancient evil allowed itself to laugh once more.

The End

Ready for the next adventure?

A Grim Situation:
Book 2 of the GrimFaerie Chronicles

AVAILABLE NOW!!

For updates about new releases, exclusive promotions, and a complimentary short story, visit the author's website and sign up for the VIP mailing list at

http://www.whitmcclendon.com

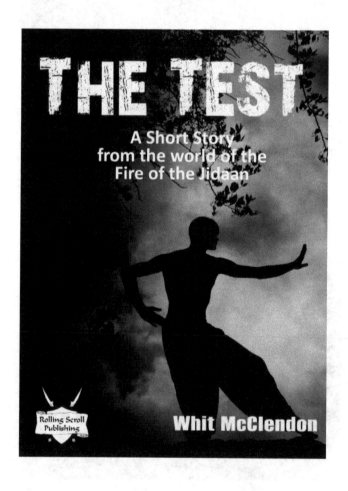

Also By Whit McClendon

Mage's Burden, Gart's Road, and A Mage Awakens, all in one action-packed volume!

Look for it on Amazon, iBooks, and BarnesandNoble.com!

About The Author

Whit McClendon was born on October 31, 1969 in Freeport, Tx. He grew up in Angleton Texas and was active in martial arts, track and field, and playing the clarinet in band. One year at Texas A & M proved that lacrosse was far more fun than electrical engineering, and he eventually graduated with a degree in Engineering Design Graphics from Brazosport College. After working in the petrochemical field as a CAD drafter for many years, Whit finally realized his life's dream of becoming a full-time martial arts instructor. He now lives with his family in Katy, Texas, plays lacrosse as often as possible, and runs Jade Mountain Martial Arts. He laughs a lot more now than he did when he worked at the engineering firm.

whitmcc@jidaan.com
www.jidaan.com
www.jmma.org

9 781732 630048